Y0-DCZ-528

ZANE GREY
RIDES AGAIN!

The master storyteller brings alive the Old West as
no other writer has ever done. He knew the
gunslingers, cowpunchers, sodbusters and lawmen
—and his unforgettable characterizations
of early Western pioneers were drawn from his own
personal experience. Here, in ROUND-UP,
he has captured them all. . . .

**ALSO BY
ZANE GREY**

BLUE FEATHER

ROUND-UP

ZANE GREY

MANOR
BOOKS
INC.

A MANOR BOOK......1976

Manor Books, Inc.
432 Park Avenue South
New York, New York 10016

Copyright, ©, 1976, by Manor Books, Inc.
All rights reserved.
Printed in the U.S.A.

ABOUT ZANE GREY

Zane Grey has been considered by many to be the master Western story writer of all times. He was born in Zanesville, Ohio and educated to the dentistry at the University of Pennsylvania. But, as was his pioneer ancestor Colonel Ebenezer Zane, who commanded Fort Henry in West Virginia during the Revolutionary War days and later founded Zanesville, he was essentially an outdoorsman at heart. During his adventurous career he roped lions in the Grand Canyon, hiked through Death Valley, mapped rivers in Mexico and fished streams never explored by anglers. He probably knew the American West as well as any writer who ever lived. Though many of his characters were fictional, the settings were authentic as he himself had seen them. He, at one time, had visited the locale of every one of his fifty-seven novels and numerous outdoor books. The grandeur of the wild ranges, the lonely mountains, the merciless desert, and natural wonders such as the Rainbow Bridge, Monument Valley, Grand Canyon and Black Mesa furnished the settings for his masterful action-packed stories.

Zane Grey also knew the gun slinger, the cowpunchers, the sodbusters, the lawmen who were part of the early West. From his own personal experience came his unforgettable characterizations of early western pioneers, cowboys and their women were far more in accord with reality than any of them suspected. My authority for this is a research just recently conducted by Professor Joseph Wheeler of George Peabody College in a doctoral dissertation which also suggests that Zane Grey's influence on American culture and thinking was much greater than any of his critics realized.

Here, in THE ROUND-UP, are some of his greatest stories and characterizations. They depict the drama and sweep of the raw West as only he could portray them.

—*Loren Grey*

RUSTLERS OF SALMON RIVER

The lone horseman rode slowly up the slope, bending far down from his saddle in the posture customary for a range rider when studying hoof tracks. The intensity of his scrutiny indicated far more than the depth or direction of these imprints in the dust.

Presently the rider sat up and turned in his saddle to look back. While pondering the situation his eagle eyes swept the far country below. It was a scene like hundreds of others etched upon his memory—a vast and rugged section of the West, differing only in the elements of color, beauty, distance and grandeur that characterized the green Salmon River Valley, the gray rolling range beyond, the dead-white plain of alkali and the purple saw-toothed peaks piercing the sky in the far distance.

That the tracks of the stolen Watrous thoroughbreds would lead over the range into Montana had been the trailer's foregone conclusion. But that the mysterious horse thieves had so far taken little care to conceal their tracks seemed proof of how brazen this gang had become. On the other hand Dale Brittenham reflected that he was a wild-horse hunter—that a trail invisible to most men would be like print to him.

3

He gazed back down the long slope into Idaho, pondering his task, slowly realizing that he had let himself in for a serious and perhaps deadly job.

It had taken Dale five hours to ride up to the point where he now straddled his horse, and the last from which he could see the valley. From here the stage road led north over the divide into the wild-timbered range.

The time was about noon of an early summer day. The air at that height had a cool, sweet tang, redolent of the green pines and the flowered mountain meadows. Dale strongly felt the beauty and allurement of the scene, and likewise a presentiment of trouble. The little mining town of Salmon, in the heyday of its biggest gold producing year, 1886, nestled in a bend of the shining white and green river. Brittenham had many enemies down there and but few friends. The lonely life of a wild-horse hunter had not kept him from conflict with men. Whose toes might he not step upon if he tracked down these horse thieves? The country was infested with road agents, bandits, horse thieves; and the wildest era Idaho had ever known was in full swing.

"I've long had a hunch," Dale solilquized broodingly. "There's men down there, maybe as rich and respectable as Watrous himself, who're in cahoots with these thieves . . . Cause if there wasn't, thick slick stealin' couldn't be done."

The valley shone green and gold and purple under the bright sun, a vast winding range of farms, ranches, pastures, leading up to the

4

stark Sawtooth Mountains, out of which the river glistened like a silver thread. It wound down between grassy hills to meander into the valley. Dale's gaze fastened upon an irregular green spot and a white house surrounded by wide sweeping pastures. This was the Watrous ranch. Dale watched it, conscious of a pang in his heart. The only friendship for a man and love of a woman he had ever known had come to him there. Leale Hildrith, the partner of Jim Watrous in an extensive horse-breeding and trading business, had once been a friend in need to Brittenham. But for Hildrith, the wild-horse hunter would long before have taken the trail of the thieves who regularly, several times a year, plundered the ranches of the valley. Watrous had lost hundreds of horses.

"Dale, lay off," Hildrith had advised impatiently. "It's no mix of yours. It'll lead into more gunplay, and you've already got a bad name for that. Besides, there's no telling where such a trail might wind up."

Brittenham had been influenced by the friend to whom he owed his life. Yet despite his loyalty, he wondered at Hildrith's attitude. It must surely be that Hildrith again wanted to save him from harm, and Dale warmed to the thought. But when, on this morning, he had discovered that five of Edith Watrous's thoroughbreds, the favorite horses she loved so dearly, had been stolen, he said no word to anyone at the ranch and set out upon the trail.

At length Brittenham turned his back upon the valley and rode on up the slope toward the timber line, now close at hand. He reached the straggling firs at a point where two trails branched off the road. The right one led along the edge of the timber line and on it the sharp tracks of the shod horses showed plainly in the dust.

At this junction Dale dismounted to study the tracks. After a careful scrutiny he made the deduction that he was probably two hours behind the horse thieves, who were plainly lagging along. Dale found an empty whiskey bottle, which was still damp and strong with the fumes of liquor. This might in some measure account for the carelessness of the thieves.

Dale rode on, staying close to the fir trees, between them and the trail, while he kept a keen eye ahead. On the way up he had made a number of conjectures, which he now discarded. This branching off the road puzzled him. It probably meant that the horse thieves had a secret rendezvous somewhere off in this direction. After perhaps an hour of travel along the timber belt Dale entered a rocky region where progress was slow, and he came abruptly upon a wide, well-defined trail running at right angles to the one he was on. Hundreds of horses had passed along there, but none recently. Dale got off to reconnoiter. He had stumbled upon something that he had never heard the riders mention—a trail which wound up the mountain slope over an exceedingly rough route. Dale followed it until he had an appreciation of what a hard climb, partly on foot, riders must put themselves to, coming up from the valley. He realized that here was the outlet for horse thieves operating on the Salmon and Snake River ranges of Idaho. It did not take Dale long to discover that it was a one-way trail. No hoof tracks pointing down!

"Well, here's a rummy deal!" he ejaculated. And he remembered the horse traders who often drove bands of Montana horses down into Idaho and sold them all the way to Twin Falls and Boise. Those droves of horses came down the stage road. Suddenly Dale arrived at an exciting conclusion. "By thunder! Those Montana horses are stolen, too. By the same gang—a big gang of slick horse thieves. They steal way down on the Montana ranges— drive up over a hidden trail like this to some secret place where they meet part of their outfit who've been stealin' in Idaho...Then they switch herds...And they drive down, sellin' the Montana horses in Idaho and the Idaho horses in Montana... Well! The head of that outfit has got brains. Too many to steal Jim Watrous's fine blooded stock! That must have been a slip...But any rider would want to steal Edith Watrous's horses!"

Returning to his mount, Dale led him in among the firs and rocks, keeping to the line of the new trails but not directly upon it. A couple of slow miles brought him to the divide. Beyond that the land sloped gently, the rocks and ridges merged into a fine open forest. His view was unobstructed for several hundred yards. Bands of deer bounded away from in front of Dale to halt and watch, their long ears

7

erect. Dale had not hunted far over that range. He knew the Sawtooth Mountains only up to Thunder Mountain. His wild-horse activities had been confined to the desert and low country toward the Snake River. Therefore he had no idea where this trail would lead him. Somewhere over this divide, on the eastern slope, lived a band of Palouse Indians. Dale knew some of them and had hunted wild horses with them. He had befriended one, Nalook, to the extent of saving him from a jail sentence. From that time Nalook had been utterly devoted to Dale, and had rendered him every possible service.

By mid-afternoon Brittenham was far down on the forested table-land. He meant to stick to the trail as long as there was light enough to see. His saddlebag contained meat, biscuits, dried fruit and salt. His wild-horse hunts often kept him weeks on the trail, so his present pursuit presented no obstacles. Nevertheless, as he progressed he grew more and more wary. He expected to see a log cabin in some secluded spot. At length he came to a brook that ran down from a jumble of low bluffs and followed the trail. The water coursed in alternate eddies and swift runs. Beaver dams locked it up into little lakes. Dale found beaver cutting aspens in broad daylight, which attested to the wildness of the region. Far ahead he saw rocky crags and rough, gray ridgetops. This level, open forest would not last much farther.

Suddenly Brittenham's horse shot up his ears and halted in his tracks. A shrill neigh came faintly to the rider's ears. He peered ahead through the pines, his nerves tingling.

But Dale could not make out any color or movement, and the sound was not repeated. This fact somewhat allayed his fears. After a sharp survey of his surroundings Dale led his horse into a clump of small firs and haltered him there. Then, rifle in hand, he crept forward from tree to tree. This procedure was slow work, as he exercised great caution.

The sun sank behind the fringe of timber on the high ground and soon shadows appeared in thick parts of the forest. Suddenly the ring of an axe sent the blood back to Alex's heart. He crouched down behind a pine and rested a moment, his thoughts whirling. There were campers ahead, or a cabin; and Dale strongly inclined to the conviction that the horse thieves had stopped for the night. If so, it meant they were either far from their rendezvous or taking their time waiting for comrades to join them. Dale pondered the situation. He must be decisive, quick, ruthless. But he could not determine what to do until he saw the outfit and the lay of the land.

Wherefore he got up, and after a long scrutiny ahead he slipped from behind the tree and stole on to another. He repeated this move. Brush and clumps of fir and big pines obstructed any considerable survey ahead. Finally he came to less thick covering on the ground. He smelled smoke. He heard faint indistinguishable sounds. Then a pinpoint of fire gleamed through the thicket in front of him. Without more ado Dale dropped on all fours and crawled straight for that light. When he got to the brush and peered through his heart gave a great leap at the sight of Edith Watrous's horses staked out on a grassy spot.

Then he crouched on his knees, holding the Winchester tight, trying to determine a course of action. Various plans flashed through his mind. The one he decided to be the least risky was to wait until the thieves were asleep and quietly make away with the horses. These thoroughbreds knew him well. He could release them without undue excitement. With half a night's start he would be far on the way back to the ranch before the thieves discovered their loss. The weakness of this plan lay in the possibility of a new outfit joining this band. That, however, would not deter Dale from making the attempt to get the horses.

It occured to him presently to steal up on the camp under cover of the darkness and if possible get close enough to see and hear the robbers. Dale lay debating this course and at last yielded to the temptation. Dusk settled down. The night hawks wheeled and uttered their guttural cries overhead. He waited patiently. When it grew dark he crawled around the thicket and stood up. A bright campfire blazed in the distance. Dark forms moved to and fro across the light. Off to the left of Dale's position there appeared to be more cover. He sheered off that way, lost sight of the campfire, threaded a careful approach among trees and brush, and after a long detour came up behind the camp, scarcely a hundred yards distant. A big pine tree dominated an open space lighted by the campfire. Dale selected objects to use for cover and again sank to his hands and knees. Well he knew that the keenest of men were easier to crawl upon than wild horses at rest. He was like an Indian. He made no more noise than a snake. At intervals he peered above the grass and low bush. He heard voices and the sputtering of the fire. He rested again. His next stop would be behind a wind-fall that now obscured the camp. Drawing a deep breath, he crawled on silently without looking up. The grass was wet with dew.

A log barred Dale's advance. He relaxed and lay quiet, straining his ears.

"I tell you, Ben, this hyar was a damn fool job," spoke up a husky-voiced individual. "Alec agrees with me."

"Wal, I shore do," corroborated another man. "We was drunk."

"Not me. I never was more clear-headed in my life," replied the third thief, called Ben. His reply ended with a hard chuckle.

"Wal, if you was, no one noticed it," returned Alec sourly. "I reckon you roped us into a mess."

"Aw hell! Big Bill will yelp with joy."

"Mebbe. Shore he's been growin' overbold these days. Makin' too much money. Stands too well in Halsey an' Bannock, an' Salmon. Cocksure no one will ever find our hole-up."

"Bah! That wouldn't faze Big Bill Mason. He'd bluff it through."

"Aha! Like Henry Plummer, eh? The coldest proposition of a robber that ever turned a trick. He had a hundred men in his outfit. Stole damn near a million in gold. High respected citizen of Montana. Mayor of Alder Gulch.... All the same he put his neck in the noose!"

"Alec is right, Ben," Spoke up the third member in his husky voice. "Big Bill is growin' wild. Too careless. Spends too much time in town. Gambles. Drinks... Someday some foxy cowboy or hoss hunter will trail him. An' that'll be about due when Watrous finds his blooded horses gone."

"Wal, what worries me more is how Hildrith will take this deal of yours," said Alec. "Like as not he'll murder us."

Brittenham sustained a terrible shock. It was like a physical rip of his flesh. Hildrith! These horse thieves spoke familiarly of his beloved friend. Dale grew suddenly sick. Did not this explain Leale's impatient opposition to the trailing of horse thieves?

"Ben, you can gamble Hildrith will be wild," went on Alec. "He's got sense if Big Bill hasn't. He's Watrous's pardner, mind you. Why, Jim Watrous would hang him."

"We heard talk this time that Hildrith was goin' to marry old Jim's lass. What a hell of a pickle Leale will be in!"

"Fellers, he'll be all the stronger if he does grab thet hoss-lovin' gurl. But I don't believe he'll be so lucky. I seen Edith Watrous in town with thet cowboy Les Crocker. She shore makes a feller draw his breath hard. She's young an' she likes the cowboys."

"Wal, what of that? If Jim wants her to marry his pardner, she'll have to."

"Mebbe she's a chip off the old block. Anyway, I've knowed a heap of women an' thet's my hunch . . . Hildrith will be as sore as a bunged-up thumb. But what can he do? We got the hosses."

"So we have. Five white elephants! Ben, you've let *your* cravin' for fine hoss-flesh carry you away."

An interval of silence ensued, during which Dale raised himself to peer guardedly over the log. Two of the thieves sat with hard red faces in the glare of the blaze. The third had his back to Dale.

"What ails *me*, now I got 'em, is can I keep 'em," this man replied. "Thet black is the finest hoss I ever seen."

"They're all grand hosses. An' thet's all the good it'll do you." retorted the leaner of the other two.

"Ben, them thoroughbreds air known from Deadwood to Walla Walla. They can't be sold or rid. An' shore as Gawd made little apples, the stealin' of them will bust Big Bills' gang."

"Aw, you're a couple of yellow pups," rejoined Ben contemptuously. "If I'd known you was goin' to show like this I'd split with you an' done the job myself."

"Uhuh! I recollect now thet *you* did the watchin' while Steve an' me stole the horses. An' I sort of recollect dim like thet you talked big about money while you was feedin' us red likker."

"Yep, I did—an' I had to get you drunk. Haw! Haw!"

"On purpose? Made us trick the outfit an' switch to your job, huh?"

"Yes, on purpose."

"So... How you like this on purpose, Ben?" hissed Alec, and swift as a flash he whipped out a gun. Ben's hoarse yell of protest died in his throat with the bang of the big Colt.

The bullet went clear through the man and hit the log near Dale. He ducked instinctively, then sank down again, tense and cold.

"My Gawd! Alec, you bored him," burst out Steve.

"I shore did. The damned bullhead!... An' thet's our out with Hildrith. We're gonna need one. I reckon Big Bill won't hold it hard agin us."

Dale found himself divided between conflicting courses—one, to shoot these horse thieves in their tracks, and a stronger one, to stick to his first plan and avoid unnecessary hazard. Wherewith he noiselessly turned and began to crawl away from the log. He had to worm under spreading branches. Despite his care, a dead limb, invisible until too late, caught on his long spur, which gave forth a ringing metallic peal. At the sudden sound, Dale sank prone, his blood congealing in his veins.

"Alec! You hear that?" called Steve, his husky voice vibrantly sharp.

"By Gawd I did!.... Ring of a spur! I know thet sound."

"Behind the log!"

The thud of quick footsteps urged Dale out of his frozen inaction. He began to crawl for the brush.

"There Steve! I hear someone crawling. Smoke up thet black patch!"

Gunshots boomed. Bullets thudded all around Dale. Then one tore through his sombrero, leaving a hot sensation in his scalp. A gust of passion intercepted Dale's desire to escape. He whirled to his knees. Both men were outlined distinctly in the firelight. The foremost stood just behind the log, his gun spouting red. The other crouched peering into the darkness. Dale shot them both. The leader fell hard over the log, and lodged there, his boots beating a rustling tattoo on the ground. The other flung his gun high and flopped as if his legs had been chopped from under him.

Brittenham leaped erect, working the lever of his rifle, his nerves strung like wires. But the engagement had ended as quickly as it had begun. He strode into the campfire circle of light. The thief, Ben, lay on his back, arms wide, his dark visage distorted ghastly. Dale's impulse was to search these men, but resisting it he hurriedly made for the horses. The cold sick grip on his vitals eased with hurried action, and likewise the fury.

Presently he reached the grasy plot where the horses were staked out. They snorted and thumped the ground.

"Prince," he called and whistled.

The great stallion whinnied recognition. Dale made his way to the horse. Prince was blacker than the night. Dale laid gentle hands on him and talked to him. The other horses quieted down.

"Jim . . . Jake . . . Ringspot . . . Bluegrass," called Dale, and repeated the names as he passed among the horses. They all were pets except Jade, and she was tempermental. She had to be now. Presently Dale untied her long stake rope, and after that the ropes of the other horses. He felt sure Prince and Jim would follow him anywhere, but he did not want to risk it then.

He led the five horses back, as nearly as he could, on the course by which he had approached the camp. In the darkness the task was not easy. He chose to avoid the trail, which ran somewhere to the left. A tree and a thicket here and there he recognized. But he was off his direction when his own horse nickered to put him right again.

"No more of that, Hoofs," he said, when he found his animal. Cinching his saddle, he gathered up the five halters and mounted. "Back trail yourself, old boy!"

The Waltrous' horses were eager to follow, but the five of them abreast on uneven and obstructed ground held Dale to a slow and watchful progress. Meanwhile, as he picked his way, he began figuring the situation. It was imperative that he travel all night. There seemed hardly a doubt that the three thieves would be joined by others of their gang.

Anyone save a novice could track six horses through a forest. Dale meant to be a long way on his back trail before dawn. The night was dark. He must keep close to the path of the horse thieves so that he would not get lost in this forest. Once out on the stage road he could make up for slow travel.

Trusting to Hoofs, the rider advanced, peering keenly into the gloom. He experienced no difficulty in leading the thoroughbreds; indeed they often slacked their halters and trampled almost at his heels. They knew they were homeward bound, in the charge of a friend. Dale hoped all was well, yet could not rid himself of a contrary presentiment. The reference of one of the horse thieves to Ben's double-crossing their comrades seemed to Dale to signify that the remaining outfit might be down in the Salmon River Valley.

At intervals Dale swerved to the left far enough to see the trail in the gloom. When he could hear the babble of the brook he knew he was going right. In due time he worked out of the open forest and struck the grade, and eventually got into the rocks. Here he had to follow the path, but he endeavored to keep his tracks out of it. And in this way he found himself at length in a shallow, narrow gulch, the sides of which appeared unscalable. If it were short, all would be well; on the other hand he distrusted a long defile, where it would be perilous if he happened to encounter any riders. They would scarcely be honest riders.

The gulch was long. Moreover it narrowed

and was dark as pitch except under the low walls. Dale did not like Hoofs's halting. His trusty mount had the nose and ears of the wild horses he had hunted for years.

"What ails you, hoss?" queried Dale.

Finally Hoofs stopped. Dale, feeling for his ears, found them erect and stiff. Hoofs smelled or heard something. It might be a bear or a cougar, both of which the horse disliked exceedingly. It might be more horse thieves, too. Dale listened and thought hard. Of all things, he did not want to retrace his steps. While he had time then, and before he knew what menaced further progress, he dismounted and led the horses as far under the dark wall as he could get them. Then he drew their heads up close to him and called low, "Steady, Prince...Jade, keep still...Blue, hold now...."

Hoofs stood at his elbow. It was Dale's voice and hand that governed the intelligent animals. Then as a low trampling roar swept down the gully they stood stiff. Dale tingled. Horses coming at a forced trot! They were being driven when they were tired. The sound swelled, and soon it was pierced by the sharp calls of riders.

"By thunder!" muttered Dale, aghast at the volume of sounds. "My hunch was right! ...Big Bill Mason has raided the valley...Must be over a hundred head in that drove."

The thudding, padded roar, occasionally emphasized by an iron-shod hoof ringing on stone, or a rider's call, swept down the gully. It

18

was upon Dale before he realized the drove was so close. He could see a moving, obscure mass coming. He smelled dust. "Git in thar!" shouted a weary voice. Then followed a soft thudding of hoofs on sand. Dale's situation was precarious, for if one of his horses betrayed his whereabouts, there would be riders sheering out for strays. He held the halters with his left hand, and pulled his rifle from its saddle sheath. If any of these raiders bore down on him, he would be forced to shoot and take to flight. But his thoroughbreds, all except Jade, stood like statues. She champed her bit restlessly. Then she snorted. Dale hissed at her. The moment was one to make him taut. He peered through the gloom, expecting riders to loom up, and he had the grim thought that it would be death for them, then there followed a long moment of sustained suspense, charged with incalculable chance.

"Go along there, you lazy hawses," called a voice.

The soft thumping of many hoofs passed. Voices trailed back. Dale relaxed in immeasurable relief. The driving thieves had gone by. He thought then for the first time what a thrilling thing it was going to be to return these thoroughbreds to Edith Watrous.

Hard upon that came the thought of Leale Hildrith—his friend. It was agony to think that Leale was involved with these horse thieves. On the instant Dale was shot through with the memory of his debt to Hildrith—of that terrible day when Hildrith had found him out on the range, crippled, half-starved and frozen, and had, at the risk of his own life, carried Dale through the blizzard to the safety of a distant shelter. A friendship had sprung up between the two men, generous and careless on Hildrith's part, even at times protective. In Dale had been engendered a passionate loyalty and gratitude, almost a hero worship for the golden-bearded Hildrith.

What would come of it all? No solution presented itself to Dale at the moment. He must meet situations as they arose, and seek in every way to protect his friend.

Toward sunset the following day Dale Brittenham rode across the clattering old bridge, leading the Watrous thoroughbreds into the one and only street of Salmon. The dusty horses, five abreast, trotting at the end of long halters, would have excited interest in any Western town. But for some reason that puzzled Dale, he might have been leading a circus or a band of painted Indians.

Before he had proceeded far, however, he grasped that something unusual accounted for the atmosphere of the thronged street. Seldom did Salmon, except on a Saturday night, show so much activity. Knots of men, evidently in earnest colloquy, turned dark faces in Dale's direction; gaudily dressed dance-hall girls, black-frocked gamblers, and dusty-booted, bearded miners crowded out in the street to see Dale approach; cowboys threw up their sombreros and let out their cracking whoops; and a throng of excited youngsters fell in behind Dale, to follow him.

Dale began to regret having chosen to ride through town, instead of fording the river below and circling to the Watrous ranch. He did not like the intense curiosity manifested by a good many spectators. Their gestures and words, as he rode by, he interpreted as more curiosity than welcome at his return with the five finest horses in Idaho.

When Dale was about halfway down the wide street, a good friend of his detached himself from a group and stepped out.

"Say, Wesley, what'n hell's all this hubbub about?" queried Brittenham as he stopped.

"Howdy, Dale," returned the other, offering his hand. His keen eyes flashed like sunlight on blue metal and a huge smile wrinkled his bronzed visage. "Well, if I ain't glad to see you I'll eat my shirt... Just like you, Dale, to burst into town with thet bunch of hosses!"

"Sure, I reckoned I'd like it. But I'm gettin' leery. What's up?"

"Hoss thieves raided the river ranches yesterday," replied the other swiftly. "Two hundred head gone!... Chamberlain, Trash, Miller—all lost heavy. An' Jim Watrous got cleaned out. You know, lately Jim's gone in for cattle buyin' an' his riders were away somewhere. Jim lost over a hundred head. He's ory-eyed. An' they say Miss Edith was heartbroke to lose hers. Dale, you sure got the best of her other beaux with this job."

"Stuff!" ejaculated Dale, feeling the hot blood in his cheeks, and he sat up stiffly. "Wes, damn you—"

"Dale, I've had you figgered as a shy

21

hombre with girls. Every fellow in this valley, except you, has cocked his eyes at Edith Watrous. She's a flirt, we all know . . . Listen, I been achin' to tell you my sister Sue is a friend of Edith an' she says Edith likes you pretty well. Hildrith only has the inside track cause of her father. I'm tellin' you, Dale."

"Shut up, Wes. You always hated Hildrith, an' you're wrong about Edith."

"Aw, hell! You're scared of her an' you overrate what Hildrith did for you once. Thet's all. This was the time for me to give you a hunch. I won't shoot off my chin again."

"An' the town's all het-up over the horse-thief raid?"

"You bet it is. Common talk runs thet there's some slick hombre here who's in with the hoss thieves. This Salmon Valley has lost nigh on to a thousand head in three years. An' everyone of the big raids come at a time when the thieves had to be tipped off."

"All big horse-thief gangs work that way," replied Dale, ponderingly. Wesley was trying to tell him that suspicion had fallen upon his head. He dropped his eyes as he inquired about his friend Leale Hildrith.

"Humph! In town yesterday, roarin' louder than anybody about the raid. Swore this stealin' had to be stopped. Talked of offerin' ten thousand dollars reward—that he'd set an outfit of riders after the thieves. You know how Leale raves. He's in town this mornin', too."

"So long, Wes," said Dale soberly, and was about to ride on when a commotion broke the

22

ring of bystanders to admit Leale Hildrith himself.

Dale was not surprised to see the golden-bearded, booted-and-spurred partner of Watrous, but he did feel a surprise at a fleeting look in Hildrith's steel-blue eyes. It was a flash of hot, murderous amazement at Dale there with Edith Watrous thoroughbreds. Dale understood it perfectly, but betrayed no sign.

"Dale! You son-of-a-gun." burst out Hildrith in boisterous gladness, as he leaped to seize Dale's hand and pumped it violently. His apparent warmth left Dale cold, and bitterly sad for his friend. "Fetched Edith's favorites back! How on earth did you do it, Dale? She'll sure reward you handsomely. And Jim will throw a fit...Where and how did you get back these horses?"

"They were stolen out of the pasture yesterday mornin' about daylight," replied Dale curtly. "I trailed the thieves. Found their camp last night. Three men, callin' themselves Ben, Alec an' Steve. They were fightin among themselves. Ben tricked them, the other two said. An' one of them shot him...They caught me listenen' and forced me to kill them."

"You killed them!" queried Hildrith hoarsely, his face turning pale. His eyes held a peculiar oscillating question.

"Yes. An' I didn't feel over-bad about it, Leale," rejoined Dale with sarcasm. "Then I wrangled the horses an' rode down."

"Where was this?"

"Up on the mountain, over in Montana somewhere. After nightfall I sure got lost. But I hit the stage road...I'll be movin' along, Leale."

"I'll come right out to the ranch," replied Hildrith, and hurried through the crowd.

"Open up there," called Dale to the staring crowd. "Let me through."

As he parted the circle and left it behind, a taunting voice cut the silence. "Cute of you, Dale, fetchin' the high-steppers back. Haw! Haw!"

Dale rode on as if he had not heard, though he could have shot the owner of that mocking voice. He had been implicated in this horse stealing. Salmon was full of shifty-eyed, hard-lipped men who would have had trouble in proving honest occupations. Dale had clashed with some of them, and he was hated and feared. He rode on through town and out into the country. He put the horses to a brisk trot, as he wanted to reach the Watrous ranch ahead of Hildrith.

Dale was appalled at the dual character of the man to whom he considered himself so deeply indebted, whom he had looked on as a friend and loved so much. It was almost impossible to believe. Almost every man in the valley liked Leale Hildreth and called him friend. The women loved him, and Dale felt sure, despite Wesley's blunt talk, that Edith Watrous was one of them. And if she did love him, she was on the way to disgrace and misery. Leale, the gay, handsome blade, not yet thirty, so good natured and kindly, big hearted and open handed, was secretly nothing but a low down horse thief. Dale had hoped against hope that when he saw Hildrith the disclosures of the three horse thieves would somehow be disproved. But that had not happened. Hildrith's eyes, in only a flash, had betrayed him. Dale suffered the degradation of his own disillusion. Yet the thought of Edith's unhappiness hurt him even more.

He had not gotten anywhere in his perplexed and bewildered state of mind when the bronze and gold hills of the Watrous ranch loomed before him. From the first day he had ridden up to it. Dale had loved this great ranch with its big, old weather beaten house nestled among the trees up from the river, its smooth, shinning hills bare to the gray rocks and timber line, its huge field of corn and alfalfa green as emerald, its level range spreading away from the river gateway to the mountains. From that very day, too, Dale had loved the lithe, free-stepping, roguish-eyed daughter of Jim Watrous, a melancholy and disturbing fact that he strove to banish from his consciousness. Her teasing and tormenting, her fits of cold indifference and her resentment that she could not make him bend to her like her other admirers, her flirting before his eyes plainly to make him jealous—all these weaknesses of Edith's did not equal in sum her kindness to him, and the strange inexplicable fact that when she was in trouble she always came to him.

As Dale rode around the grove into the green square where the gray ranch house stood on its slope, he was glad to see that Hildrith had not arrived. Three men on saddled horses standing near the porch had sighted him. Crowding to the high steps, they could be heard exclaiming. Then gray-haired Jim Watrous, stalwart of build and ruddy of face, descended down a step to call lustily, "Edith! Rustle out here. Quick!"

Dale halted on the green below the porch. It was going to be a hard moment. Watrous and his visitors could not disturb him. But Edith!.... Dale heard the swift patter of light feet—then a little scream, sweet, high-pitched, that raised a turbulent commotion in his breast.

"Oh Dad!...My horses!" she exclaimed in ecstasy, and she clasped her hands.

"They sure are, lass," replied Watrous gruffly.

"Ha! Queer Brittenham should fetch them," added a man back of Watrous.

In two leaps Edith came down the high steps, supple as a cat, and bounded at Dale, her bright hair flying, her dark eyes shining.

"Dale! Dale!" she cried rapturously, and ran to clasp both hands around his arm. "You old, wild-horse hunter! You darling!"

"Well, I'll stand for the first," said Dale, smiling down at her.

"You'll stand for that—and hugs—and kisses when I get you alone, Dale Brittenham...You've brought back my horses! My heart was broken. I was crazy. I couldn't eat or sleep...Oh, it's too good to be true! Oh Dale, I can never thank you enough."

She left him to throw her arms around Prince's dusty neck and to cry over him. Watrous came slowly down the steps, followed by his three visitors, two of whom Dale knew by sight. He bent the eyes of a hawk upon Dale.

"Howdy, Brittenham. What have you got to say for yourself?"

"Horses talk, Mr. Watrous, same as money," replied Dale cooly. He sensed the old horse trader's doubt and dismay.

"They sure do, young man. There's ten thousand dollars' worth of horseflesh. To Edith they're priceless. What's your story?"

Dale told it briefly, omitting the description of the horse-thief's trail and the meeting upon it with the raided stock from the valley. He chose to save these details until he had had more time to ponder over them.

"Brittenham, you can prove those three horse thieves are dead—an' that you made away with two of them?" queried Watrous tensely.

"Prove!" ejaculated Dale, sorely nettled. "I could prove it—certainly, sir, unless their pards came along to pack them away...But my word should be proof enough, Mr. Watrous."

"I reckon it would be, for me, Brittenham," returned the rancher hastily. "But this whole deal has a queer look...This gang of horse thieves has an accomplice—maybe more than one—right here in Salmon."

"Mr. Watrous, I had the same thought," said Dale shortly.

27

"Last night, Brittenham, your name was whispered around in this connection."

"That doesn't surprise me. Salmon is full of crooked men. I've clashed with some. I've only a few friends an'—"

Edith whirled to confront her father with pale face and blazing eyes.

"Dad! Did I hear aright? What did you say?"

"I'm sorry, lass. I told Brittenham he was suspected of bein' the go-between for this horse-thief gang."

"For shame, father! It's a lie. Dale Brittenham would not steal, let alone be a cowardly informer."

"Edith, I didn't say I believed it," rejoined Watrous, plainly upset. "But it's bein' said about town. It'll fly over the range. An' I thought Brittenham should know."

"You're right, Mr. Watrous," said Dale. "Thank you for tellin' me."

The girl turned to Dale, evidently striving for composure.

"Come, Dale. Let us take the horses out."

She led them across the green toward the lane. Dale had no choice but to follow, though he desperately wanted to flee. Before the men were out of range of his acute hearing, one of them exclaimed to Watrous, "Jim, he didn't deny it!"

"Huh! Did you see his eyes?" returned the rancher shortly. "I'd not want to be in the boots of the man who accuses him to his face."

"Here comes Hildrith, drivin' as if the devil was after him."

Dale heard the clattering buckboard, but he did not look. Neither did Edith. She walked with her head down, deep in thought. Dale dared to watch her, conscious of inexplicable feelings.

The stable boy, Joe, ran out to meet them, with a face that was a study in inexpressible wonder and delight. Edith did not relinquish the halters until she had led the horses up the incline into the wide barn.

"Joe, water them first," she said. "Then wash and rub them down. Take a look at their hoofs. Feed them a little alfalfa. And watch them every minute till the boys get back."

"Yes, Miss Edith, I shore will," he replied eagerly. "We done had words they'll be hyar by dark."

Dale dismounted and removed saddle and bridle from his tired horse.

"Let Joe watch your horse, Dale. I want to talk to you."

Dale leaned against some bales of hay, not wholly from weariness. He had often been alone with Edith Watrous, but never like this.

"Reckon I ought to—to clean up," he stammered, removing his sombrero. "I—I must look a mess."

"You're grimy and worn, yes. But you look pretty proven and good to me, Dale Brittenham...What's that hole in your hat?"

"By thunder! I forgot about that. It's a bullet hole."

"Oh! So close...Who shot it there, Dale?"

"One of the horse thieves."

"It was self-defense, then?"

"You bet it was."

"I've hated your shooting scrapes, Dale," she rejoined earnestly. "But here I see I'm squeamish—and unreasonable...Only the reputation you have—your readiness to shoot—that's all I never liked about it."

"I'm sorry. But I can't help that," replied Dale, turning his sombrero round and round with restless hands.

"You needn't be sorry this time...Dale, look me straight in the eye."

Thus so earnestly urged, Dale had to comply. Edith appeared pale of face and laboring under suppressed emotion. Her dark eyes had held many expressions for him, mostly roguish and coquettish, and sometimes blazing, but at this moment they were beautiful with a light, a depth he had never seen in them before. And it challenged him with a truth he had always driven from his consciousness that he loved this bright-haired girl.

"Dale, I was ashamed of Dad," she said. "I detest that John Stafford. He is the one who brought the gossip from town—that you were implicated in this raid. I don't believe it."

"Thanks Edith. It's good of you."

"Why didn't you say something?" she asked spiritedly. "You should have cussed Dad roundly."

"I was sort of flabbergasted."

"Dale, if this whole range believed you were a horse thief, I wouldn't. Even if your faithful Nalook believed it—though he never would."

"No. I reckon that Indian wouldn't believe bad of me."

"Nalook thinks heaps of you, Dale—and—and that's one reason why I do—too."

"Heaps?"

"Yes, heaps."

"I'd never have suspected it."

"Evidently you never did. But it's true. And despite your—your rudeness—your avoidance of me, now is the time to tell it."

Dale dropped his eyes again, sorely perturbed and fearful that he might betray himself. Edith was not bent on conquest now. She appeared roused to championship of him, and there was something strange and soft about her that was new and bewildering.

"I never was rude," he denied stoutly.

"We won't argue about that now," she went on hurriedly. "Never mind about me and my petty vanity...I'm worried about this gossip. It's serious, Dale. You'll get into trouble and go gunning for somebody—unless I keep you from it. I'm going to try...Will you take a job riding for me—taking care of my horses?"

"Edith!...I'm sure obliged to you for that offer. But Watrous wouldn't see it."

"I'll make him see it."

"Hildrith?...He wouldn't like that idea—now."

"Leale will like anything I want him to."

"Not this time."

"Dale, *will* you ride for me?" she queried impatiently.

"I'd like to—if—if... Well, I'll consider it."

31

"If you would that'd stop this gossip more than anything I can think of . . . I'd like it very much, Dale. I'll never feel safe about my horses again, not until these thieves are rounded up. If you worked for me I could keep you here—out of that rotten Salmon. And you wouldn't be going on those long, wild-horse hunts."

"Edith, you're most amazin' kind an'—an' thoughtful all of a sudden." Dale could not quite keep a little bitter surprise out of his voice.

She blushed vividly. "I might have been all that long ago—if you had let me," she responded.

"Who am I to aspire to your kindness?" he said almost coldly. "But even if I wasn't a poor wild-horse hunter, I'd never run after you like these—these—"

"Maybe that's one reason why . . . well, never mind," she interrupted, with a hint of her old roguishness. "Dale, I'm terribly grateful to you for bringing back my horses. I know you won't take money. I'm afraid you'll refuse the job I offered . . . So, Mister Wild-Horse Hunter, I'm going to pay you as I said I would—back at the house."

"No!" he cried, suddenly weak. "Edith, you wouldn't be so silly—so—Aw, it's just the devil in you."

"I'm going to Dale."

Her voice drew him as well as her intent; and forced to look up, he was paralyzed to see her bending to him, her face aglow, her eyes alight. Her hands flashed upon his shoulders—slipped back—and suddenly pressed like bands of steel. Dale somehow recovered strength to stand up and break her hold.

"Edith, you're out of—your head," he said huskily.

"I don't care if I am. I always wanted to, Dale Brittenham. This was a good excuse ...And I'll never get another."

The girl's face was scarlet as she drew back from Dale, but it paled before she concluded her strange speech.

"You're playin' with me—you darned flirt," he blurted out.

"Not this time, Dale," she replied soberly, and then Dale grasped that something deeper and hitherto unguessed had followed hard on her real desire to reward him for his service.

"It'll be now or never, Dale...for this morning at breakfast I gave in at last to Dad's nagging—and consented to marry Leale Hildrith."

"Then it'll be never, my strange girl," replied Dale hoarsely, shot through with anguish for Edith and his treacherous friend. "I—I reckoned this was the case...You love Leale?"

"I think—I do," replied Edith, somewhat hesitantly. "He's handsome and gay. Everybody loves Leale. You do. All the girls are mad about him. I—I love him, I guess...But it's mostly Dad. He hasn't given me any peace for a year. He's set on Hildrith. Then he thinks I ought to settle down—that I flirt—that I have all his riders at odds with each other on my account...Oh, it made me furious."

"Edith, I hope you will be happy."

"A lot *you* care, Dale Brittenham."

"I cared too much. That was the trouble."

"*Dale*!...So that was why you avoided me?"

"Yes, that was why, Edith."

"But you are as good as any man."

"You're a rich rancher's daughter. I'm a poor wild-horse hunter."

"Oh! As if that made any difference between friends."

"Edith, it does," he replied sadly. "An' now they're accusin' me of being a horse thief ....I'll have to kill again."

"No! You mustn't fight," she cried wildly. "You might be shot...Dale, promise me you'll not go gunning for anyone."

"That's easy, Edith. I promise."

"Thanks, Dale...Oh, I don't know what's come over me." She dropped her head on his shoulder. "I'm glad you told me. It hurts—but it helps somehow. I—I must think."

"You should think that you must not be seen—like this," he said gently.

"I don't care," she flashed, suddenly aroused. Edith's propensity to change was one of her bewildering charms. Dale realized he had said the wrong thing and he shook in her tightening grasp. "You've cheated me, Dale, of a real friendship. And I'm going to punish you. I'm going to keep my word, no matter what comes of it...Oh, you'll believe me a flirt—like Dad and all of these old fools that think I've kissed these beaux of mine. But

34

I haven't—well, not since I was a kid. Not even Leale!...Dale, you might have kissed me if you'd had any sense."

"Edith, have *you* lost all sense—of—of—" he choked out.

"Of modesty?...I'm not in the least ashamed." But her face flamed as she tightened her arms around him and pressed sweet cool lips to his cheek. Dale was almost unable to resist crushing her in his arms. He tried, weakly, to put her back. But she was strong, and evidently in the grip of some emotion she had not calculated upon. For her lips sought his and their coolness turned to sweet fire. Her eyelids fell heavily. Dale awoke to spend his hunger for love and his renunciation in passionate response.

That broke the spell which had moved Edith.

"Oh, Dale!" she whispered, as she wrenched her lips free. "I shouldn't have...Forgive me...I was beside myself."

Her arms were sliding from his neck when quick footfalls and the ring of spurs sounded in the doorway. Dale looked up to see Hildrith, livid under his golden beard, with eyes flaring, halting at the threshold.

"What the hell!" he burst out incredulously.

Dale's first sensation was one of blank dismay, and as Edith, with arms dropping, drew back, crimson faced, he sank against the pile of bales like a guilty man caught in some unexplainable act.

"Edith, what did I see?" demanded Hildrith in jealous wrath.

"Not very much! You were too late. Why do you slip up on people like that?" the girl returned with a tantalizing laugh. She faced him, her blush and confusion vanishing. His strident voice no doubt roused her imperious spirit.

"You had your arms around Dale?"

"I'm afraid I had."

"You kissed him?"

"Once...No, twice, counting a little one," returned this amazing creature. Dale suffered some kind of torture only part of which was shame.

"Well, by heaven!" shouted Hildrith furiously. "I'll beat him half to death for that."

Edith intercepted him and got between him and Dale. She pushed him back with no little force. "Don't be a fool, Leale. It'd be dangerous to strike Dale. Listen...."

"I'll call him out," shouted her lover.

"And get shot for your pains. Dale has killed half a dozen men...Let me explain."

"You can't explain a thing like this."

"Yes, I can. I admit it looks bad, but it really isn't... When Dale brought my horses back, I was so crazy with joy that I wanted to hug and kiss him. I told him so. But I couldn't before Dad and all those men. When we came out here I—I tried to, but Dale repulsed me—"

"Edith! Do you expect me to believe that?" queried Hildrith.

"Yes. It's true...But the second time I succeeded—and you almost caught me in the act."

"You damned little flirt!"

"Leale, I wasn't flirting. I wanted to kiss Dale; I was in rapture about my horses. And before that Dad and those men hinted Dale was hand and glove with these horse thieves. I hated that. It excited me. Perhaps I was out of my head. Dale said I was. But you shall not blame him. It was my fault."

"Oh, hell!" fumed Hildrith in despair. "Do you deny the poor beggar is in love with you?"

"I certainly do deny that," she retorted, and her gold-tan cheeks flamed red.

"Well, he is. Anybody could see that."

"I didn't. And if it's true he never told me."

Hildrith began to pace the barn. "Good God! Engaged to marry me for half a day, and you do a brazen thing like that... Watrous is sure right. You need to be tied down. Playing fast and loose with every rider on the range! Coaxing your Dad to set our marriage day three months off!... Oh, you drive me mad. I'll tell you young woman, when you *are* my wife...."

"Don't insult me, Mr. Hildrith," interrupted Edith coldly. "I'm not your wife yet... I was honest with you, because I felt sure you'd understand. I'm sorry I told you the truth, and I don't care whether you believe me or not."

With her bright head erect, she walked past Hildrith, avoiding him as he reached for her, and she was deaf to his entreaties.

"Edith, I'll take it all back," he cried after her. But so far as Dale could see or hear she made no response. Hildrith turned away from

the door, wringing his hands. It was plain
that he worshipped the girl, that he did not
trust her, that he was inordinately suspicious,
that for an accepted lover he appeared the
most wretched of men. Dale watched him,
seeing him more clearly in the revelation of
his dual nature. Just how far Hildrith had
gone with this horse-stealing gang, Dale did
not want to know. Dale did see that his
friend's redemption was possible—that if he
could marry this girl, and if he could be
terribly frightened with possible exposure, he
might be weaned from whatever association
he had with Mason, and go honest and make
Edith happy. It was not a stable conviction,
but it gripped Dale. He had his debt to pay to
Hildrith and a glimmering of a possible way
to do it formed in his mind. Even at that
moment, though, he felt the ax of disillusion
and reality at the roots of his love for this man.
Hildrith was not what he had believed him.
But that would not deter Dale from paying his
debt a thousandfold. Lastly, if Edith Watrous
loved this man, Dale felt that he must save
him.

Hildrith whirled upon Dale. "So this is how
you appreciate what I've done for you, Dale.
You made love to my girl. You damned
handsome ragamuffin—you worked on
Edith's sympathy! You've got me into a hell of
a fix."

"Leale, you sure are in a hell of a fix,"
replied Dale with dark significance.

"What do you mean?" queried Hildrith
sharply, with a quick uplift of head.

"You're one of Big Bill Mason's gang," rejoined Dale deliberately.

Hildrith gave a spasmodic start, as if a blade had pierced his side. His jaw dropped and his face blanched to an ashen hue under his blond beard. He tried to speak, but no words came.

"I sneaked up on the camp of those three horse thieves. I listened. Those low-down thieves—Ben, Alec, Steve—spoke familiarly of you. Alec an' Steve were concerned over what you'd do about the theft of the Watrous' horses. Ben made light of it. He didn't care. They talked about Big Bill. An' that talk betrayed you to me... Leale, you're the range scout for Mason. You're the man who sets the time for these big horse raids."

"You know!... Oh, my God!" cried Hildrith abjectly.

"Yes, I know that an' more. I know the trail to Mason's secret rendezvous. I was on that trail an' saw this last big drove of stolen horses pass by. I figured out how Mason's gang operates. Pretty foxy, I'll say. But it was too good, too easy, too profitable. It couldn't last."

"For God's sake, Dale, don't squeal on me!" besought Hildrith, bending over Dale with haggard, clammy face. "I've money. I'll pay you well—anything...."

"Shut up! Don't try to buy me off, or I'll despise you for a yellow cur... I didn't say I'd squeal on you. But I do say you're a madman to think you can work long at such a lowdown game."

"Dale, I swear to God this was my last deal. Mason forced me to one more, a big raid which was to be his last in this valley. He had a hold on me. We were partners in a cattle business over in Montana. He roped me into a rustling deal before I knew what it actually was. That was three years ago, over in Kalispel. Then he found a hiding place—a box canyon known only to the Indians—and that gave him the idea of raiding both Montana and Idaho ranges at the same time, driving to the canyon and there changing outfits and stolen horses. While a raid was on over there, Mason made sure to be in Bannock or Kalispel, and he roared louder than anyone at the horse thieves. He had the confidence of all the ranchers over there. My job was the same here in the Salmon Valley. But I fell in love with Edith and have been trying to break away."

"Leale, you say you swear to God this was your last deal with Mason?"

"Yes, I swear it. I have been scared to death. I got to thinking it was too good to last. I'd be found out. Then I'd lose Edith."

"Man, you'd not only lose her. But you'd be shot—or worse, you'd be hanged. These ranchers are roused. Watrous is ory-eyed, so Wesley told me. They'll organize an' send a bunch of Wyomin' cowboys out on Mason's trail. I'll bet that's exactly what Watrous is talkin' over now with these visitors."

"Then it's too late. They'll find me out. God! Why didn't I have some sense?"

"They won't find you out if you quit.

Absolutely quit! I'm the only man outside the Mason gang who knows. If some of them are captured an' try to implicate you, it wouldn't be believed. I'll not give you away."

"Dale, by heaven, that's good of you," said Hildrith hoarsely. "I did you an injustice. Forgive me...Dale, tell me what to do. I'm in your hands. I'll do anything. Only save me. I wasn't cut out for a horse thief. It's galled me. I've been sick after every raid. I haven't the guts. I've learned an awful lesson."

"Have you any idea how Edith would despise you, if she knew?"

"That's what makes me sweat blood. I worship the very ground she walks on."

"Does she love you?"

"Oh, Lord, I don't know now. I thought so. She said she did. But she wouldn't...She promised to marry me. Watrous wants her settled. If she will marry me, I know I can make her love me."

"Never if you continued to be a two-faced, dirty, lousy, yellow dog of a horse thief," cried Dale forcefully. "You've got to perform a miracle. You've got to change. That's the price of my silence."

"Dale, I'm torn apart...What use to swear? You know I'll quit—and go straight all my life. For Edith! What man wouldn't? You would if she gave herself...any man would. Don't you see?"

"Yes, I see that, an' I believe you," replied Dale, convinced of the truth in Hildrith's agony. "I'll keep your secret, an' find a way

41

to save you if any unforseen thing crops up...An' that squares me with you, Leale Hildrith."

Swift, light footsteps that scattered the gravel cut short Hildrith's impassioned gratitude. Edith startled Dale by appearing before them, her hand at her breast, her face white as a sheet, her eyes blazing.

Hildrith met her on the incline, exclaiming, "Why, Edith! Running back like that! What's wrong?"

She paid no heed to him, but ran to Dale, out of breath and visibly shaking.

"Oh—Dale—" she panted. "Stafford sent—for the sheriff!...They're going to—arrest you."

"Stafford? Who's he? That man in the black coat?"

"Yes. He's lately got in with Dad...cattle. It's his outfit of cowboys coming...He's hard as nails."

"Are they here?"

"Will be directly. I tore loose from Dad and ran all the way...Oh, Dale, what will you do?" She was unconscious of her emotion, and she put an appealing hand upon Dale's arm. Dale had never seen her like that, nor had Hildrith. They were deeply struck each according to his reception of her white-faced, earnest demeanor.

"Edith, you can bet I won't run," declared Dale grimly. "Thank you, girl, all the same...Don't take this so—so strangely. Why, you're all upset. They can't arrest me."

Hildrith drew back from the wide door. He

appeared no less alarmed and excited than Edith. "They're coming, Dale," he said thickly. "Bayne and Stafford in the lead. That sheriff has it in for you, Dale. Only last night I heard him swear he'd jail you if you came back. It's ticklish business. What'll you do?"

"I'm sure I don't know," returned Dale with a laugh.

Edith besought him, "Oh, Dale, don't kill Bayne!... for my sake!"

"If you brace up, I reckon maybe I can avoid that."

Dale led his horse out of the barn, down the runway into the open. Then he stepped aside to face the advancing men, now nearly across the wide court. The dark garbed Stafford was talking and gesticulating vehemently to a stalwart, booted man. This was the one officer that Salmon supported, and it had been said of him that he knew which side of the law to be on. Watrous and three other men brought up the rear. They made no bones about sheering off to the side. Stafford, however, a swarthy and pompous man, evidently accustomed to authority, remained beside Bayne.

"Hey, you," called out Dale, far from civilly. "If you want to talk with me—that's close enough."

Hildrith, to Dale's surprise, came down in the incline, and took up a stand beside Dale.

"What you mean by this turkey-strutting?" he demanded, and his simulation of resentment would have deceived anyone but Dale.

"Hildrith, we got business with Brittenham," declared Bayne harshly.

43

"Well, he's my friend, and that concerns me."

"Thanks Leale," interposed Dale. "But let me handle this. Bayne, are you looking for me?"

"I sure am."

"At whose instigation?"

"Mr. Stafford, here. He sent for me, an' he orders you arrested."

Watrous broke in to say nervously, "Brittenham, I advised against this. I have nothing to do with it. I don't approve of resorting to law on the strength of gossip. If you'll deny any association with horse thieves, that will do for me. If your word is good to Edith, it ought to be for me."

"Jim Watrous, you're a fool," rasped out Stafford. "Your daughter is apparently infatuated with this—this..."

"Careful!" cut in Dale. "You might say the wrong thing. An' leave Miss Edith's name out of this deal. Stafford, what's your charge against me?"

"I think you're one of this horse-raiding gang," declared Stafford stoutly, though he turned pale.

"On what grounds?"

"I wasn't influenced by gossip, sir. I base my suspicion on your fetching back those thoroughbred horses. They must have been driven off by mistake. Any horse thief would know they couldn't be ridden or sold in Montana or Idaho. They'd be recognized. So you fetched them back because it was good

44

business. Besides, it'd put you in better with Watrous, and especially his...."

"Shut up! If you speak of that girl again I'll shoot your leg off," interrupted Dale, "an' you can gamble on this, Stafford, if I don't shoot you anyhow it'll be the only peg on which you can hang a doubt of my honesty."

"You insolent ruffian!" ejaculated Stafford, enraged and intimidated. "Arrest him, Sheriff."

"Brittenham, you'll have to come with me," spoke up Bayne with an uneasy cough. "You appear to be a talker. You'll get a chance to talk in court at Twin Falls."

"You're tryin' to go through with it?" asked Dale derisively.

"I say you're under arrest."

"What's *your* charge?"

"Same as Mr. Stafford's."

"But that's ridiculous, Bayne. You can't arrest a man for bringing back stolen horses. There's not the slightest case against me. Stafford has heard gossip in town—where half the population is crooked. How do I know an' how do you know that Stafford himself is not the big hand in this horse-stealin' gang? There's some big respectable rancher on this range who stands in with the thieves. Why do you pick on a poor wild-horse hunter? A ragamuffin, as he has called me. Look at my boots! Look at my saddle! If I was the go-between, wouldn't I have better equipment? You're not very bright, Bayne."

"Aw, that's all bluff. Part of your game. An'

you've sure pulled it clever around here for three years."

While Dale had prolonged this argument, his mind had been conceiving and fixing upon a part he wanted to play. It would have been far easier but for Edith's inexplicable importunity. She had awakened to something strange and hitherto unrevealed. It must have been pity, and real sincerity and regret come too late. Then the girl had always been fair in judging something between others. If Dale had had an inkling it was anything else, he never could have made the sacrifice, not even to save Hildrith. But she loved Hildrith; she would become his wife, and that surely meant his salvation. Dale felt that ignominy, a bad name thrust upon him, and acknowledged by his actions, could not make much difference to him. He was only a wild-horse hunter. He could ride away to Arizona and never be heard of again. Still he hated the thing he felt driven to do.

Then Edith stepped into the foreground, no longer the distraught girl who had arrived there a few moments ago to warn Dale. Had she read his mind? That suspicion affected him more stirringly than anything yet that had happened.

"Sheriff Bayne, you must not try to arrest Dale without proof," she said earnestly.

"I'm sorry, lady. It's my duty. He'll get a fair trial."

"Fair!" she exclaimed scornfully. "When this arrest is so unfair! Bayne, there's some-

thing wrong—something dishonest here—
and it's not Dale."

"Edith, don't say more," interposed her
father. "You're overwrought."

Hildrith strode to her side, hurried in
manner, dark and strained of face.

"Leale, why don't you speak up for Dale?"
she queried, and her eyes blazed upon him
with a marvelously penetrating and strange
look.

"Bayne, let Dale off," Hildrith said huskily.
"Don't make a mistake here. You've no
proof—and you can't arrest him."

"Can't! Why the hell can't I?" rejoined the
sheriff.

"Because he won't let you. Good God, man,
haven't you any mind?"

"Humph! I've got mind enough to see
there's somethin' damn funny here. But it
ain't in me...Brittenham, you're under arrest. Come on, now, no buckin'.'"

As he made a step forward Dale's gun
gleamed blue and menacing.

"Look out, Bayne! If you move a hand I'll
kill you," he warned.

He backed cautiously down the court, leading his horse to one side.

"I see what I'm up against here, an' I'm
slopin'," went on Dale. "Stafford, you had it
figured. Watrous, I engineered that raid...
Edith; I fetched your horses back because I
was in love with you." A strange laugh
followed his words.

Dale backed across the square to the lane,

where he leaped into his saddle and spurred swiftly out of sight.

Dale's campfire that night was on a bend of the brook near where he had surprised the three horse thieves, and had recovered the Watrous thoroughbreds.

Upon riding away from the Watrous ranch he had halted in Salmon long enough to buy supplies, then he had proceeded down the river to a lonely place where he had rested his horse and slept. By dawn he was climbing the mountain into Montana, and by sundown that night he was far down the horse-thief trail.

Even though Dale had branded himself by shouldering Hildriths guilt, he had determined to find Big Bill Mason's rendezvous and evolve a plan to break up the horse-thief band. Born of his passion at riding away from the Watrous Ranch a fugitive, leaving Edith to regret her faith in him, this plan seemed to loom as gigantic and impossible after the long hours of riding and thinking. But he would not abandon it.

"Stafford and Bayne will send a big outfit after me," he muttered as he sat before his little campfire. "An' I'll lead them to Mason's hiding place. Failin' thet, I'll go down on the range below Bannock an' get the ranchers there to raise a big posse of cowboys. One way or another I'm goin' to break up Mason's gang."

Dale had not thought of that in the hour of his sacrifice for Hildrith and Edith. He had meant to take his friend's ignominy and ride away from Idaho forever. But two things had operated against this. First, the astounding and disturbing fact that Edith Watrous, in her stress of feeling, had betrayed not only faith in him but more real friendship than she had ever shown; and secondly, his riding away in disgrace would leave the Mason gang intact, free to carry on their nefarious trade. He was the man for the job. If he broke up the gang, it would remove the stain from his name. Not that he would ever want to or dare to go back to the Watrous Ranch! But there was a tremendous force in the thought that he might stand clean and fine again in Edith Watrous's sight. How strangely she had reacted to that situation when her father and the others had confronted him! What could she have meant when she said there was something wrong, something dishonest there in that climax? Could she have had a glimmering of the truth? This thought was so distrubing that it made Dale catch his breath. Edith was a resource-ful, strong-minded girl, once she became aroused. On reflection, however, he eased away that doubt, and also the humanly weak joy at a possible indestructible faith in him. No! He felt sure Hildrith would be safe. Once the Mason outfit was broken up, with the principals killed and the others run out of the country, Hildrith would be safe, and Edith's happiness would be assured.

In the hours past, Dale had, in the excite-ment of his flight, believed that he could kill his love for Edith Watrous and forget her. This proved to be an illusion, the recognition of which came to him beside his lonely campfire. He would love her more, because his act had been something big and for her sake, and in his secret heart he would know that if she could be told the truth, she would see her faith justified, and whatever feeling she had for him would be intensified.

He saw her dark proud eyes and her white face in the opal glow of his fire. And having succumbed to that he could not help but remember her boldness to reward him, her arms and her kiss and, most poignant of all, the way she had been betrayed by her impulse, how that kiss had trapped her into emotion she had not intended. Was it possible that he had had this chance for Edith Watrous and had never divined it? The thought was torture, and he put it from him, assuring himself that the girl's actions had been the result of her gratitude and joy at the return of her beloved horses.

The fire died down to ruddy coals; the night wind began to seep through the grass and brush; four-footed prowlers commenced their questing. Standing erect, Dale listened. He heard his horse cropping the grass. A brooding solitude lay upon the forest.

He made his bed close under the side of a fallen pine, using his saddle for a pillow. So many nights of his life he had lain down to look up at the open dark sky with its trains of stars. But this night the stars appeared closer and they seemed to talk to him. He was conscious that his stern task, and the circumstances which had brought it about, had heightened all his faculties to a superlative degree. He seemed a vastly different man, and he conceived that it might develop that he would revel in what fate had set him to do.

At last he fell asleep. During the night he awoke several times, and the last time, which was near dawn and nippingly cold, he got up and kindled a fire. All about him rose dark gray forest wall, except in the east, where a pale brightening betokened dawn.

It was Dale's custom to cook and eat a hearty breakfast, so that he could go long on this meal if he had to. His last task before saddling was to obliterate signs of his camp. Then, with light enough to see clearly, he mounted and was off on his perilous quest.

All the way Dale had kept off the main trail. It would take an Indian or a wild-horse hunter to track him. He traveled some few paces off the horse-thief trail, but kept it in sight. And every mile or so he would halt, dismount, and walk a few steps away from his horse to listen. In that silent forest he could have heard a sound at a considerable distance.

By sunrise he was down out of the heavy timber belt and riding out upon a big country of scaly rock and immense thickets of evergreen and cedar, with only an occasional large pine. The brook disappeared—probably dried up, or sunk into the earth. The trail led on straight as a beeline, for a while.

The sun rose high, and grew hot. With the morning half spent, he figured that he had traveled fifteen miles from his last camp. Occasionally he had glimpses of the lower range, gray and vast and dim below. The trail turned west, into more rugged plateaus and away from the descent. But presently, beyond a long fringe of evergreen thicket, he saw the peculiar emptiness that proclaimed the presence of a void.

Dale knew before he reached it that he had come upon the hole in the ground where Big Bill Mason had his hideout. Leaving the trail, Dale rode to a little higher ground, where a gray stone eminence, less thickly overgrown, seemed to offer easy access to the place. Here he dismounted and pushed his way through the evergreens. At once he emerged upon a point, suddenly to stand rooted to the spot.

"What a wonderful place," he exclaimed, as he grasped the fact that his sight commanded. He stood upon the rim of a deep gorge a mile long and half as wide. On all sides, the walls sheered down a thousand feet, gray and craggy, broken and caverned, lined by green benches, and apparently unscalable. Of course trails led in and out of this hole, but Dale could not see where. The whole vast level bottomland was as green as an emerald. At each end, where the gorge narrowed, glistened a lake. All around the rims stood up a thick border of evergreens, which screened the gorge from every side. Hunters and riders could pass near there without ever guessing the presence of such a concealed pocket in the mountain plateau.

"Ahuh. No wonder Mason can steal horses wholesale," soliloquised Dale. "All he had to do was to hide his tracks just after he made a raid."

Dale reflected that the thieves had succeeded in this up to the present time. However, any good tracker could sooner or later find this rendezvous for resting and shifting droves of horses. Dale was convinced that Stafford and Watrous would send out a large outfit of riders as soon as they were available.

It struck Dale singularly that he could not see an animal or a cabin in the gorge below. But undoubtedly there were points not visible to him from this particular location. Returning to his horse, he decided to ride around the gorge to look for another trail.

He found, after riding for a while, that although the gorge was hardly more than three or four miles in circumference, to circle it on horseback or even on foot, a man would have to travel three times that far. There were canyon offshoots from the main valley and these had to be headed.

At the west side Dale found one almost as long as the gorge itself. But it was narrow. Here he discovered the first sign of a trail since he had left the main one. And this was small, and had never been traveled by a drove of horses. It led off to the south toward Bannock. Dale deliberated a moment. If he were to risk going down to investigate, this trail about halfway between the lakes at each end, should be the one for him to take. Certainly it did not show much usage. At length he rode down, impelled by a force that seemed to hold less of reason than of presentiment.

It grew steep in the notch and shady, following a precipitous water course. He had to get off and lead his horse. Soon trees and brush obstructed his view. The trail was so steep that he could not proceed slowly, and before he surmised that he was halfway down, he emerged into the open to see a beautiful narrow valley, richly green, enclosed by timbered slopes. A new cabin of peeled logs stood in the lea of the north side. He saw cattle, horses and finally a man engaged in building a fence. If Dale had encountered an individual laboring this way in any other locality he would have thought him a homesteader. It was indeed the most desirable place to homestead and ranch on a small scale that Dale had ever seen in his hunting trips.

The man saw Dale just about as quickly as Dale had seen him. Riding by the cabin, where a buxom woman and some children peeped out fearfully, Dale approached the man. He appeared to be a sturdy, thick-set farmer, bearded and sharp-eyed. He walked forward a few steps and stopped significantly near a shiny rifle leaning against the fence. When Dale got close enough, he recognized him.

"Well, Rogers, you son-of-a-gun! What're you doin' down here?"

"Brittenham! By all thet's strange. I might ask you the same," was the hearty reply, as he offered a horny hand. Two years before Dale had made the acquaintance of Rogers back in the Sawtooth range.

"When'd you leave Camus Creek?" he asked.

"This spring. Fine place thet, but too cold. I was snowed in all winter. Sold out to a Mormon."

"How'd you happen to locate in here?"

"Just by accident. I went to Bannock, an' from there to Halsey. Liked thet range country. But I wanted to be high, where I could hunt an' trap as well as homestead. One day I hit the trail leadin' in here. An' you bet I located pronto."

"Before ridin' out in the big valley?"

"Yes. But I saw it. What a range! This was big enough for me. If I'm not run out, I'll get rich here in five years."

"Then you located before you found out you had neighbors?"

"What do you know about them?" queried Rogers, giving Dale a speculative glance.

"I know enough."

"Brittenham, I hope to heaven you're not in thet outfit."

"No. An' I hope the same of you. Have you got wise yet to Mason's way of operatin'?"

"Mason! You don't mean the rancher an' horse trader Bill Mason?"

"So help me! Big Bill—the biggest horse thief in this country."

"If thet's true, who can a man trust?"

"It's true, Rogers, as you can find out for yourself by watchin'. Mason runs a big outfit. They split. One operates in Idaho, the other in Montana. They drive the stolen horses up here an' switch men an' herds. They sell the

Montana stock over in Idaho an' the Idaho stock over on the Montana ranges."

"Hell you say! Big idee an' sure a bold one. I savvy now why these men politely told me to pull up stakes an' leave. But I had my cabin up an' my family here before they found out I'd located. Then I refused to budge. Reed, the boss of the outfit, rode down again last week. Offered to buy me out. I thought thet strange. But he didn't offer much, so I refused to sell. He said his boss didn't want any homesteaders in here."

"Rogers, they'll drive you out or kill you," said Dale.

"I don't believe it. They're bluffin'. If they murdered me, it'd bring attention to this place. Nobody knows of it. I haven't told about it yet. My wife would, though, if they harmed me."

"This gang wouldn't hesitate to put you all out of the way. They just don't take you seriously yet. Think they can scare you out."

"Not me, Brittenham. How'd you come to know about this horse stealin' an' to find this hole?"

Dale told him about the theft of the Watrous thoroughbreds, how he had trailed the robbers up the mountains, what happened there and lastly about the big raid that followed hard the same day.

"I'll tell you, Rogers. I got blamed for bein' the scout member of Mason's outfit. It made me sore. I left Salmon in a hurry, believe me. My aim in findin' this hole is to organize a big posse of cowboys an' break up Mason's gang."

"Humph! You ain't aimin' to do much, at all."

"It'll be a job. There's no tellin' how many outfits Mason runs. It's a good bet thet his ranch outfit is honest an' don't suspect he's a horse thief. I'll bet he steals his own horses. If I can raise a hard-fightin' bunch an' corral Mason's gang all here in this hole... To catch them here—thet's the trick. I'd reckon they'll be stragglin' in soon. It doesn't take long to sell a bunch of good horses. Then they'd hide here, gamblin' an' livin' fat until time for another raid... Rogers, breakin' up this outfit is important to you. How'd you like to help me?"

"What could I do? Remember I'm handicapped with a wife an' two kids."

"No fightin' an' no risk for you. I'd plan for you to watch the valley, and have some kind of signs I could see from the rim to tell me when the gang is here."

"Get down an' come in," replied the homesteader soberly. "We'll talk it over."

"I'll stop a little while. But I mustn't lose time."

"Come set on the porch. Meet the wife an' have a bite to eat... Brittenham, I think I'll agree to help you. As for signs... there is the only place on the rim from which you can see my valley an' cabin. I've a big white cowhide thet I could throw over the fence. You could see it much farther than thet. If you did see it, you'd know the gang was here."

"Just the trick, Rogers. An' no risk to you,"

replied Dale with satisfaction. He unsaddled Hoofs and let him free on the rich grass. Then he accompanied Rogers to the cabin, where he spent a restful hour. When he left, Rogers walked with him to the trail. They understood one another and were in accord on the plan to break up Mason's band. Dale climbed on foot to the rim, his horse following, and then rode east to the point designated by the homesteader. Rogers watched for him and waved.

Across the canyon Dale located a curve in the wall which partly enclosed a large area black with horses. He saw cattle, too, and extensive gardens, and far up among the trees, yellow cabins admidst the green. He rode back to Rogers' trail and headed for Bannock, keen and grim over his project.

The trail zigzagged gradually down toward lower country. Dale was always vigilant. No moving object escaped him. But there was a singular dearth of life along this scantily timbered eastern mountain slope. Toward late afternoon he found himself in broken country again, where the trail wound between foothills. It was dark when he rode into Bannock.

This town, like Salmon, was in the heyday of its productivity. And it was considerably larger. Gold and silver mining were its main assets, but there was some cattle trade, and extensive business in horses, and the providing of supplies for the many camps in the hills. Gambling halls of the period, with all their manifest and hidden evils, flourished flagrantly.

A miner directed Dale to a stable where he

left his horse. Here he inquired about his Indian friend, Nalook. Then he went uptown to find a restaurant. He did not expect to meet anyone who knew him unless it was the Indian. Later that contingency would have to be reckoned with. Dale soon found a place to eat. Next to him at the lunch counter sat a red-faced cowboy who answered his greeting civilly.

"How's the hash here?" asked Dale.

"Fair to middlin'... Stranger hereabouts, eh?"

"Yep. I hail from the Snake River country."

"I see you're a range rider, but no cowman."

"You're a good guesser. My job is horses."

"Bronco buster, I'll bet."

"Nope. But I can an' do break wild horses."

"Reckon you're on your way to Halsey. There's a big sale of Idaho stock there tomorrow."

"Idaho horses. You don't say?" ejaculated Dale, pretending surprise. "I hadn't heard of it."

"Wal, I reckon it wasn't advertised over your way," replied the cowboy with a short laugh. "An' when you buy fine horses at half their value, you don't ask questions."

"Cowboy, you said a lot. I'm goin' to have a look at thet bunch. How far to Halsey?"

"Two hours for you, if you stretch leather. It takes a buckboard four."

Dale then attended to the business of eating, but that did not keep his mind from functioning actively. It staggered him to think that it was possible Mason had the brazen nerve to sell stolen Idaho horses not a hundred miles across the line.

"How about buckin' the tiger?" asked Dale's acquaintance as they went out into the street.

"No gamblin' for me, cowboy. I like to look on, though, when there's some big bettin'."

"I seen a game today. Poker. Big Bill Mason won ten thousand at Steen's. You should have heard him roar. 'Thet pays up for the bunch of hosses stole from me the other day.'"

"Who's Big Bill Mason?" asked Dale innocently.

"Wal, he's about the whole cheese down Halsey way. Got his hand in most everythin'. I rode for him a spell."

"Does he deal much in horses?"

"Not so much as with cattle. But he always runs four or five hundred head on his ranch."

Presently Dale parted from the cowboy and strolled along the dimly lit street, peering into the noisy saloons, halting near groups of men, and listening. He spent a couple of hours that way, here and there picking up bits of talk. No mention of the big steal of Idaho horses came to Dale's ears. Still, with a daily stagecoach between the towns it was hardly conceivable that some news had not sifted through to Bannock.

Before leaving town, Dale bought a new shirt and a scarf. He slept that night in the barn where he had his horse put up. A pile of hay made a better bed than Dale was used to. But for a disturbing dream about Edith Watrous, in which she visited him in jail, he slept well. Next morning he shaved and donned his new garments, after which he went into the town for breakfast. He was wary this morning. Early though the hour, the street was dotted with vehicles, and a motley string of pedestrians passed to and fro on the sidewalks.

Dale had a leisurely and ample breakfast, after which he strolled in the street to the largest store and entered, trying to remember what it was that he had wanted to purchase.

"Dale!" A voice transfixed him. He looked up to be confronted by Edith Watrous.

A red-cheeked, comely young woman accompanied Edith, and looked at Dale with bright, curious eyes. He stammered confusedly in answer to Edith's greeting.

"Susan, this is my friend Dale Brittenham." Edith introduced him hurriedly. "Dale—Miss Bradford...I came over here to visit Susan."

"Glad to meet you, Miss," returned Dale, doffing his sombrero awkwardly.

"I've heard about you," said the girl, smiling at Dale. But evidently she saw something was amiss for she turned to Edith and said, "You'll want to talk, I'll do my buying."

"Yes, I want to talk to my friend Dale Brittenham," agreed Edith seriously. Her desire to emphasize the word *friend* could not be mistaken. She drew him away from the entrance of the store to a more secluded space. Then: "Dale!" Her voice was low and full of suppressed emotion. Pale, and with eyes dark with scorn and sorrow, she faced him.

"How'd you come over here?" he queried, regaining his coolness.

"Nalook drove me in the buckboard. He returned to the ranch after you left. We got here last night."

"I'm sorry you had the bad luck to run into me."

"Not bad luck, Dale. I followed you. I was certain you'd come here. There's no other town to go to."

"Followed me? Edith, what for?"

"Oh, I don't know yet... After you left I had a quarrel with Leale and Dad. I upbraided them for not standing by you. I swore you couldn't be a horse thief. I declared you were furious—that in your bitterness you just helped them to think badly of you."

"How could they help that when I admitted my—my guilt?"

"They couldn't—but *I* could... Dale, I know you. If you had been a real thief, you'd never—never have told me you—you loved me that last terrible moment. You couldn't. You wanted me to know. You looked bitter—hard—wretched. There was nothing low-down or treacherous about you."

"Edith, there you're wrong," returned Dale hoarsely. "For there is."

"Dale, don't kill my faith in you... Don't kill something I'm—I'm afraid...."

"It's true—to my shame an' regret."

"Oh!... So that's why you never made love to me like the other boys? You were man enough for that, at least. I'm indebted to you.

62

But I'll tell you what I've found out. If you had been the splendid fellow I thought you—and if you'd had sense enough to tell me sooner that you loved me—well—there was no one I liked better, Dale Brittenham."

"My God!—Edith, don't—I beg you—don't say thet now," implored Dale, in passionate sadness.

"I care a great deal for Leale Hildrith. But it was Dad's match. I told Leale so. I would probably have come to it of my own accord in time. Yesterday we had a quarrel. He made an awful fuss about my leaving home, so I slipped away unseen. But I'll bet he's on the way here right now."

"I hope he comes after you," said Dale, bewildered and wrenched by this disclosure.

"He'd better not...Never mind him, Dale. You've hurt me. Perhaps I deserved it. For I have been selfish and vain with my friends. To find out you're a—a thief—Oh, I hate you for making me believe it! It's just sickening. But you can't—you simply can't have become callous. You always had queer notions about range horses being free. There are no fences in parts of Idaho—Oh, see how I make excuses for you! Dale, promise me you will never help to steal another horse so long as you live."

Dale longed to fall upon his knees to her and tell her the truth. She was betrayed more than she knew. He had seen her audacious and winning innumerable times, and often angry, and once eloquent, but never so tragic and beautiful as now. It almost broke down his will. He had to pull his hand from hers—to

63

force a hateful stand utterly foreign to his nature.

"Edith, I won't lie to you—"

"I'm not sure of that," she retorted, her eyes piercing him. They had an intense transparency through which her thought, her doubt, shone like a gleam.

"Nope. I can't promise. My old wild-horse business is about played out. I've got to live."

"Dale, I'll give—lend you money, so you can go away far and begin all over again. Please, Dale?"

"Thanks, lady," he returned, trying to be laconic. "Sure I couldn't think of thet."

"You're so strange—so different. You didn't use to be like this...Dale, is it my fault you went to the bad?"

"Nonsense!" he exclaimed in sudden heat. "Reckon it was just in me."

"Swear you're not lying to me."

"All right, I swear."

"If I believed I was to blame, I'd follow you and make you honest. I ought to do it anyhow."

"Edith, I'm sure glad you needn't go to such extremes. You can't save a bad egg."

"Oh—Dale...." She was about to yield further to her poignant mood when her friend returned.

"Edie, I'd have stayed away longer," said Susan, her eyes upon them, "only if we're going to Halsey we must rustle pronto."

"Edith, are you drivin' over there?" asked Dale quickly.

"Yes. Susan's brother is coming. There's a

big horse sale on. I'm just curious to see if there will be any of Dad's horses there."

"I'm curious about that, too," admitted Dale soberly. "Good-bye, Edith...Miss Bradford, glad to meet you, an' good-bye."

Dale strode swiftly out of the store, though Edith's call acted upon him like a magnet. Once outside, with restraint gone, he fell in a torment. He could not think coherently, let alone reason. That madcap girl, fully aroused, might be capable of anything. Dale suffered anguish as he rushed down the street and to the outskirts of town where he saddled his horse and rode away down the slope to the east. There were both horsemen and vehicles going in the same direction, which he surmised was toward Halsey. Dale urged his mount ahead of them and then settled down to a steady sharp gait. He made no note of time, or the passing country. Long before noon he rode into Halsey.

The town appeared to be deserted, except for clerks in stores, bartenders at the doors of saloons, and a few loungers. Only two vehicles could be seen down the long length of the street. Dale did not need to ask why, but he did ask to be directed to the horse fair. He was not surprised to find a couple of hundred people, mostly men, congregated at the edge of town, where in an open green field several score of horses, guarded by mounted riders, grazed and bunched in front of the spectators. Almost the first horse he saw proved to be one wearing the Watrous brand.

Then Dale had a keen eye for that drove of

horses and especially the horsemen. In a country where all men packed guns, their being armed did not mean anything to casual observers. Nevertheless to Dale it was significant. They looked to him to be a seasoned outfit of hard riders. He hid Hoofs in the background and sauntered over toward the center of activities.

"Where's this stock from?" he asked one of a group of three men, evidently ranchers, who were bystanders like himself.

"Idaho. Snake River range."

"Sure some fine saddle hosses," went on Dale. "What they sellin' for?"

"None under a hundred dollars. An' goin' like hot cakes."

"Who's the hoss dealer?"

"Ed Reed. Hails from Twin Falls."

"Ahuh. Gentlemen, I'm a stranger in these parts," said Dale deliberately. "I hear there's no end of hoss business goin' on—hoss sellin', hoss buying', hoss tradin'—and hoss stealin'."

"Wal, this is hoss country," spoke up another of the trio dryly, as he looked Dale up and down. Dale's cool speech had struck them significantly.

"You all got the earmarks of range men," Dale continued curtly. "I'd ask, without pearin' too inquisitive, if any one of you has lost stock lately?"

There followed a moment of silence in which the three exchanged glances and instinctively edged closer together.

"Wal, stranger, I reckon thet's a fair question," replied the eldest, a gray-haired, keen-eyed Westerner. "Some of us ranchers down in the range have been hit hard lately."

"By what? Fire, flood, blizzard, drought—or hoss thieves?"

"I'd reckon the last, stranger. But don't forget you said it."

"Fine free country, this, where a range man can't talk right out," rejoined Dale caustically. "I'll tell you why. You don't know who the hoss thieves are. An' particular, their chief. He might be one of your respectable rancher neighbors."

"Stranger, you got as sharp a tongue as eye," returned the third member of the group. "What's your name an' what's your game?"

"Brittenham. I'm a wild-horse hunter from the Snake River Basin. My game is to get three or four tough cowboy outfits together."

"Wal, thet oughtn't be hard to do in this country, if you had reason," returned the rancher, his eyes narrowing. Dale knew he did not need to tell these men that the drove of horses before them had been stolen.

"I'll look you up after the sale," he concluded.

"My name's Strickland. We'll sure be on the lookout for you."

The three moved on toward the little crowd near the horses at that moment under inspection. "Jim, if we're goin' to buy some stock we've got to hustle," remarked one.

Dale sauntered away to get a good look at the main drove of horses. When he recognized Dusty Dan, a superb bay that he had actually straddled himself, a bursting gush of hot blood burned through his veins. Deliberately he stepped closer, until he was halted by one of the mounted guards.

"Whar you goin', cowboy?" demanded this individual, a powerful rider of mature years, clad in greasy leather chaps and dusty blouse. He had a bearded visage and deep-set eyes, gleaming under a black sombrero pulled well down.

"I'm lookin' for my hoss," replied Dale mildly.

The guard gave a slight start, barely perceptible.

"Wal, do you see him?" he queried insolently.

"Not yet."

"What kind of hoss, cowboy?"

"He's a black with white face. Wearin' a *W* brand like that bay there. He'd stand out in thet bunch like a silver dollar in a fog."

"Wal, he ain't hyar, so you can mosey back."

"Hell you say," retorted Dale, changing his demeanor in a flash. "These horses are on inspection...An' see here, Mr. Leather Pants, don't tell *me* to mosey anywhere."

Another guard, a lean, sallow-faced man, rode up to query, "Who's this guy, Jim?"

"Took him for a smart-alec cowboy."

"You took me wrong, you Montana buckeroos," interposed Dale, cool and caustic. "I'll mosey around an' see if I can pick out a big black hoss with the *W* Brand."

Dale strode on, but he heard the guard called Jim mutter to his companion, "Tip

Reed off." Presently Dale turned in time to see the rider bend from his saddle to speak in the ear of a tall dark man. Thus Dale identified Ed Reed, and without making his action marked, he retraced his steps. On his way he distinguished more *W* brands and recognized more Watrous horses.

Joining the group of buyers, Dale looked on from behind. After one survey of Big Bill Mason's right-hand man Dale estimated him to be a keen, suave villain whose job was to talk, but who would shoot on the slightest provocation.

"Well, gentlemen, we won't haggle over a few dollars," Reed was saying blandly as he waved a hairy brown hand. "Step up and make your offers. These horses have got to go."

Then the buying took on a brisk impetus. During the next quarter of an hour a dozen and more horses were bought and led away, among them Dusty Dan. That left only seven animals, one of which was the white face black Dale had spoken about to the guard, but had not actually seen.

"Gentlemen, here's the pick of the bunch," spoke up Reed. "Eight years old. Sound as a rock. His sire was blooded stock. I forget the name. What'll you offer?"

"Two hundred fifty," replied a young man eagerly.

"That's a start. Bid up, gentlemen. This black is gentle, fast, wonderful gait. A single-footer. You see how he stacks up."

"Three hundred," called Dale, who meant to

outbid any other buyers, take the horse and refuse to pay.

"Come on. Don't you Montana men know horseflesh when...."

Reed halted with a violent start and the flare of his eyes indicated newcomers. Dale wheeled with a guess that he verified in the sight of Edith Watrous and Leale Hildrith, with another couple behind them. He also saw Nalook, the Indian, at the driver's seat of the buckboard. Hildrith's face betrayed excessive emotion under control. He tried to hold Edith back. But, resolute and pale, she repelled him and came on. Dale turned swiftly so as not to escape Reed's reaction to this no doubt astounding and dangerous interruption. Dale was treated to an extraordinary expression of fury and jealousy. It passed from Reed's dark glance and dark face as swiftly as it had come.

Dale disliked the situation that he saw imminent. There were ten in Reed's gang—somber, dark-browed men, whom it was only necessary for Dale to scrutinize once to gauge their status. On the other hand the majority of spectators and buyers were not armed. Dale realized that he had to change his mind, now that Edith was there. To start a fight would be fool-hardy and precarious.

The girl had fire in her eyes as she addressed the little group.

"Who's boss here?" she asked.

"I am, Miss...Ed Reed, at your service." Removing his sombrero he made her a gallant bow. His face strong and not unhandsome in a bold way. Certainly his gaze was one of unconcealed admiration.

"Mr. Reed, that black horse with the white face belongs to me," declared Edith imperiously.

"Indeed?" replied Reed, exhibiting apparently genuine surprise. "And who're you, may I ask?"

"Edith Watrous. Jim Watrous is my father."

"Pleased to meet you...You'll excuse me, Miss Watrous, if I ask for proof that this black is yours."

Edith came around so that the horse could see her, and she spoke to him. "Dick, old boy, don't you know me?"

The black pounded the ground, and with a snort jerked the halter from the man who held him. Whinnying, he came to Edith, his fine eyes soft, and he pressed his nose into her hands.

"There!...Isn't that sufficient?" asked Edith.

Reed looked on with feigned amusement. Dale gauged him as deep and resourceful.

"Sam, fetch my hoss. I'm tired standing and I reckon this lady has queered us for other buyers."

"Mr. Reed, I'm taking my horse whether you like it or not," declared Edith forcefully.

"But, Miss Watrous, you can't do that. You haven't proved to me he belongs to you. I've seen many fine horses that'd come to a woman."

"Where did you get Dick?"

"I bought him along with the other *W*-brand horses."

"From whom?" queried Edith derisively.

"John Williams. He's a big breeder in horses. His ranch is on the Snake River. I daresay your father knows him."

Dale stepped out in front. "Reed, there's no horse breeder on the Snake River," he said.

The horse thief cooly mounted a superb bay that had been led up, and then gazed sardonically from Edith to Dale.

"Where do you come in?"

"My name is Brittenham, I'm a wild-horse hunter. I know every foot of range in the Snake between the falls an' the foothills."

"Williams' ranch is way up in the foothills," rejoined Reed easily. He had not exactly made a perceptible sign to his men, but they had closed in, and two of them slipped out of their saddles. Dale could not watch them and Reed at the same time. He grew uneasy. These thieves, with their crafty and bold leader, were masters of the situation.

"Lady, I hate to be rude, but you must let go that halter," said Reed, with an edge on his voice.

"I won't."

"Then I'll have to be rude. Sam, take that rope away from her."

"Leale, say something, can't you? What kind of a man are you, anyway?" cried Edith, turning in angry amazement to her fiance.

"What can I say?" asked Hildrith, spreading wide his hands, as if helpless. His visage

72

at the moment was not prepossessing.

"What! Why tell him you know this is my horse."

Reed let out a laugh that had bitter satisfaction as well as irony in it. Dale had to admit that the predicament for Hildrith looked extremely serious.

"Reed, if Miss Watrous says it's her horse, you can rely on her word," replied the pallid Hildrith.

"I'd take no woman's word," returned the leader.

"Dale, you know it's my horse. You've ridden him. If you're not a liar, Mr. Reed knows you as well as you know me."

"Excuse me, lady," interposed Reed. "I never saw your wild-horse hunter champion in my life. If he claims to know me, he is a liar."

"Dale!" Edith transfixed him with soul-searching eyes.

"I reckon you forget, Reed. Or you just won't own up to knowin' me. Thet's no matter . . . But the horse belongs to Miss Watrous. I've ridden him. I've seen him at the Watrous Ranch every day or so for years."

"Brittenham. Is that what you call yourself? I'd lie for her, too. She's one grand girl. But she can't rob me of this horse."

"Rob! That's funny, Mr. Reed," exclaimed Edith hotly. "You're the robber! I'll bet Dick against two bits that *you're* the leader of this horse-thief gang."

"Well, I can't shoot a girl, much less such a pretty and tantalizing one as you. But don't say that again. I might forget my manners."

"You brazen fellow!" cried Edith, probably as much incensed by his undisguised and bold gaze as by his threat. "I not only think you're a horse thief, but I call you one!"

"All right. You can't be bluffed, Edith," he returned grimly. "You've sure got nerve. But you'll be sorry, if it's the last trick I pull on this range."

"Edith, get away from here," ordered Hildrith huskily, and he plucked at her with shaking hands. "Let go that halter."

"No!" cried Edith, fight in every line of her face and form, and she backed away from Hildrith. She inadvertently drew nearer to Reed.

"But you don't realize who—what this man—"

"Do you?" she flashed piercingly.

Dale groaned in spirit. This was the end of Leale Hildrith. The girl was as keen as a whip and bristling with suspicion. The unfortunate man almost cringed before her. Then Reed rasped out, *"Rustle there!"*

At the instant that Reed's ally Sam jerked the halter out of Edith's hand, Dale felt the hard prod of a gun against his back. "Put 'em up, Britty," called a surly voice. Dale lost no time getting his hands above his head and he cursed under his breath for his haste and impetuosity. He was relieved of his gun. Then the pressure on his back ceased.

Reed reached down to lay a powerful left hand on Edith's arm.

74

"Let go!" the girl burst out angrily, and she struggled to free herself. "Oh—you hurt me! Stop, you ruffian."

"Stand still, girl!" ordered Reed, trying to hold her and the spirited horse. "He'll step on you—crush your foot."

"Ah-h!" screamed Edith, in agony, and she ceased her violent exertion to stand limp, holding up one foot. The red receded from her face.

"Take your hand off her," shouted Hildrith, reaching for a gun that was not there.

"Is that your stand, Hildrith?" queried Reed, cold and hard.

"What do you—mean?"

"It's a showdown. This jig is up. Show yellow—or come out with the truth before these men. Don't leave it to me."

"Are you drunk—or crazy?" screamed Hildrith, beside himself. He did not grasp Reed's deadly intent, whatever his scheme was. He thought his one hope was to play his accustomed part. Yet he suspected a move that made him frantic. "Let her go!...Damn your black hide—let her go!"

"Black, but not yellow, you traitor!" wrung out Reed as he leveled a gun at Hildrith. "We'll see what the boss says to this...Rustle, or I'll kill you. I'd like to do it. But you're not my man...Get over there quick. Put him on a horse, men, and get going. Sam, up with her!"

Before Dale could move, even if he had been able to accomplish anything, unarmed as he was, the man seized Edith and threw her up on

Reed's horse, where despite her struggles and cries he jammed her down in the saddle in front of Reed.

As Reed wheeled away, looking back with menacing gun, the spectators burst into a loud roar. Sam dragged the black far enough to be able to leap astride his own horse and spur away, pulling his captive into his stride. The other men, ahead of Reed, drove the unsaddled horses out in front. The swiftness and precision of the whole gang left the crowd stunned. They raced out across the open range, headed for the foothills. Edith's pealing cry came floating back.

Dale was the first to recover from the swift, raw shock of the situation. All around him milled an excited crowd. Most of them did not grasp the significance of the sudden exodus of the horse dealers until they were out of sight. Dale, nearly frantic, lost no time in finding Strickland.

"Reckon I needn't waste time now convincin' you there are some horse thieves in this neck of woods?" he spat out sarcastically.

"Brittenham, I'm plumb beat," replied the rancher, and he looked it. "In my ten years on this range I never saw the like of that...My Gawd! What an impudent rascal! To grab the Watrous girl right under our noses! Not a shot fired!"

"Don't rub it in," growled Dale. "I had to watch Reed. His man got the drop on me. A lot of slick hombres. An' thet's not sayin' half."

"We'll hang every damn one of them," shouted Strickland harshly.

"Yes. After we save the girl...Step aside here with me. Fetch those men you had...Come, both of you...Now, Strickland, this is stern business. We've not a minute to waste. I want a bunch of hard-ridin' cowboys here *pronto*. Figure quick now, while I get my horse, an' find thet Indian."

Dale ran into the lithe, dark, buckskin-clad Nalook as he raced for his horse. This Indian had no equal as a tracker in Idaho.

"Boss, you go me," Nalook said in his low voice, with a jerk of his thumb toward the foothills. Apparently the Indian had witnessed the whole action.

"Rustle, Nalook. Borrow a horse an' guns. I've got grub."

Dale hurried back, leading Hoofs. Reaching Strickland and his friends, he halted with them and waited, meanwhile taking his extra guns out of his pack.

"I can have a posse right here in thirty minutes," declared the rancher.

"Good. But I won't wait. The Indian here will go with me. We'll leave a trail they can follow on the run. Tracks an' broken brush."

"I can get thirty or more cowboys here in six hours."

"Better. Tell them the same."

Nalook appeared at his elbow. "Boss, me no find hoss."

"Strickland, borrow a horse for this Indian. I'll need him."

"Joe, go with the Indian," said Strickland. "Get him horse and outfit if you have to buy it."

"You men listen and hold your breath," whispered Dale. "This Reed outfit is only one of several. Their boss is Big Bill Mason."

The ranchers were beyond surprise or shock. Strickland snapped his fingers.

"That accounts. Dale, I'll tell you something. Mason got back to Halsey last night from Bannock," he said. "He was not himself. This morning he sold his ranch—gave it away, almost—to Jeff Wheaton. He told Wheaton he was leaving Montana."

"Where is he now?"

"Must have left early. You can bet something was up for him to miss a horse sale."

"When did Reed's outfit arrive?"

"Just before noon."

"Here's what has happened," Dale calculated audibly. "Mason must have learned thet Stafford an' Watrous was sendin' a big posse out on the trail of Mason's Idaho outfit."

"Brittenham, if this Ed Reed didn't call Hildrith to show his hand for or against that outfit, then I'm plumb deaf."

"It looked like it," admitted Dale gloomily. "I thought he was going to kill Hildrith."

"So did I. There's bad blood between them."

"Hildrith has had dealings of some kind with Reed. Remember how Reed spit out, 'We'll see what the boss says about this. . . . I'd like to kill you'? . . . Brittenham, I'd say Hildrith has fooled Watrous and his daughter, and this Mason outfit also."

Dale was saved from a reply by the approach of Nalook, mounted on a daughty mustang. He carried a carbine and wore a brass-studded belt with two guns.

"We're off, Strickland," cried Dale, kicking his stirrup straight and mounting. "Hurry your posse an' outfits. Pack light, an' rustle's the word."

Once out of the circle of curious onlookers, Dale told Nalook to take the horse thieves' trail and travel. The Indian pointed toward the foothills.

"Me know trail. Big hole. Indian live there long time. Nalook's people know hoss thieves."

"I've been there, Nalook. Did you know Bill Mason was the chief of thet outfit?"

"No sure. See him sometime. Like beaver. Hard see."

"We'd better not short-cut. Sure Reed will make for the hide-out hole. But he'll camp on the way."

"No far. Be there sundown."

"Is it that close from this side? ... All the better. Lead on, Nalook. When we hit the brush we want to be close on Reed's heels."

The Indian followed Reed's tracks at a lope. They led off the grassy lowland toward the hills. Ten miles or more down on the range to the east Dale spied a ranch, which Nalook said was Mason's. At that distance it did not look pretentious. A flat-topped ranch house, a few sheds and corrals, and a few cattle dotting the grassy range inclined Dale to the conviction that this place of Mason's had served as a blind to his real activities.

Soon Nalook led off the rangeland into the foothills. Reed's trail could have been followed in the dark. It wound through ravines and hollows between hills that soon grew high and wooded on top. The dry wash gave place to pools of water here and there, and at last a running brook, lined by grass and willows growing green and luxuriant.

At length a mountain slope confronted the trackers. Here the trail left the watercourse and took a slant up the long incline. Dale sighted no old hoof marks and concluded that Reed was making a short-cut to the rendez-vous. At intervals Dale broke branches on the willows and brush he passed, and let them hang down, plainly visible to a keen eye. Rocks and brush, cactus and scrub oak grew increasingly manifest, and led to the cedars, which in turn yielded to the evergreens.

It was about mid-afternoon when they surmounted the first bench of the mountain. With a posse from Halsey possibly only a half-hour behind, Dale slowed up the Indian. Reed's tracks were fresh in the red, bare ground. Far across the plateau the belt of pines showed black, and gray rock ridges stood up. Somewhere in that big rough country hid the thieves' stronghold.

"Foller more no good," said Nalook, and left Reed's tracks for the first time.

Dale made no comment. But he fell to hard pondering. Reed, bold outlaw that he was, would this time expect pursuit and fight, if he stayed in the country. His abducting the girl had been a desperate unconsidered impulse, prompted by her beauty, or by desire for revenge on Hildrith, or possibly to hold her for ransom, or all of these together. No doubt he knew this easy game was up for Mason. He had said as much to Hildrith. It was not conceivable to Dale that Reed would stay in the country if Mason was leaving. They had made their big stake.

Nalook waited for Dale on the summit of a ridge. "There!" he said, and pointed.

They had emerged near the head of a valley that bisected the foothills and opened out upon the range, dim and hazy below. Dale heard running water. He saw the white flags of deer in the green brush. It was a wild and quiet scene.

"Mason trail come here," said the Indian, with an expressive gesture downward.

Then he led on, keeping to the height of slope; and once over that, entered rough and thicketed land that impeded their progress. In many places the soft red and yellow earth gave way to stone, worn to every conceivable shape. There were hollows and upstanding grotesque slabs and cones, and long flat stretches, worn uneven by erosion. Evergreens and sage and dwarf cedars found lodgment in holes. When they crossed this area to climb higher and reach a plateau, the sun was setting gold over the black mountain heights. Dale recognized the same conformation of earth and rock that he had found on the south side of the robbers' gorge. Nalook's slow progress and caution brought the tight cold stretch to Dale's skin. They were nearing their objective.

At length the Indian got off his horse and tied it behind a clump of evergreens. Dale followed suit. They drew their rifles.

"We look—see. Mebbe come back," whispered Nalook. He glided on without the slightest sound or movement of foliage, Dale endeavoring to follow his example. After traversing half a mile in a circuitous route, he halted and put a finger to his nose. "Smell smoke. Tobac."

But Dale could not catch the scent. Not long afterward, however, he made out the peculiar emptiness behind a line of evergreens and this marked the void they were seeking. They kept on at a snail's pace.

Suddenly Nalook halted and put a hand back to stop Dale. He could not crouch much lower. Warily he pointed over the fringe of low evergreens to a pile of gray rocks. On the summit sat a man with his back to the trackers. He was gazing intently in the opposite direction. This surely was a guard stationed there to spy any pursuers, presumably approaching on the trail.

"Me shoot him," whispered Nalook.

"I don't know," whispered Dale in reply, perplexed. "How far to their camp?"

"No hear gun."

"But there might be another man on watch."

"Me see."

The Indian glided away like a snake. How

invaluable he was in a perilous enterprise like this! Dale sat down to watch and wait. The sun sank and shadows gathered under the evergreens. The scout on duty seemed not very vigilant. He never turned once to look back. But suddenly he stood up guardedly, and thrust his rifle forward. He took aim and appeared about to fire. Then he stiffened strangely, and jerked up as if powerfully propelled. Immediately there followed the crack of a rifle. Then the guard swayed and fell backward out of sight. Dale heard a low crash and a rattle of rocks. Then all was still. He waited. After what seemed a long anxious time, the thud of hoofs broke the silence. He sank down, clutching his rifle. But it was Nalook coming with the horses.

"We go quick. Soon night," said the Indian, and led the way toward the jumble of rocks. Presently Dale saw a trail as wide as a road. It led down. Next he got a glimpse of the gorge. From this end it was more wonderful to gaze down into, a magnificent hole, with sunset gilding the opposite wall, and purple shadows mantling the caverns, and the lake shining black.

Viewed from this angle Mason's rendezvous presented a different and more striking spectacle. This north end where Dale stood was a great deal lower than the south end, or at least the walls were lower and the whole zigzag oval of rims sloped toward him, so that he was looking up at the southern escarpments. Yet the floor of the gorge appeared level. From this vantage point the caverns and cracks in the walls stood out darkly and mysteriously, suggesting hidden places and perhaps unseen exits from this magnificent burrow. The deep indentation of the eastern side, where Mason had his camp, was not visible from any other point. At that sunset hour a mantle of gold and purple hung over the chasm. All about it seemed silent and secretive, a wild niche of nature, hollowed out for the protection of men as wild as the place. It brooded under the gathering twilight. The walls gleamed dark with a forbidding menace.

Nalook started down, leading his mustang. Then Dale noted that he had a gun belt and long silver spurs hung over the pommel of his saddle. He had taken time to remove these from the guard he had shot. This trail was open and from its zigzag corners Dale caught glimpses of the gorge, and of droves of horses. Suddenly he remembered that he had forgotten to break brush and otherwise mark their path after they had sheered off Reed's tracks.

"Hist!" he whispered. The Indian waited. "It's gettin' dark. Strickland's posse can't trail us."

"Ugh. They foller Reed. Big moon. All same day."

Thus reassured, Dale followed on, grimly fortifying himself to some issue near at hand.

When they came out into the open valley below, dusk had fallen. Nalook had been in that hole before, Dale made certain. He led away from the lake along a brook, and let his horse drink. Then he drank himself, and motioned Dale to do likewise. He went on then in among scrub oak trees to a grassy open spot where he halted.

"Mebbe a long fight," he whispered, "I'll rope the hoss." Dale removed saddle and bridle from Hoofs and tied him on a long halter.

"What do?" asked Nalook.

"Sneak up on them."

By this time it was dark down in the canyon, though still light above. Nalook led out of the trees and, skirting them, kept to the north wall. Presently he turned and motioned Dale to lift his feet, one after the other, to remove his spurs. The Indian hung them in the crotch of a bush. Scattered trees of larger size began to loom up on this higher ground. The great black wall stood up rimmed with white stars. Dim lights glimmered through the foliage and gradually grew brighter. Nalook might have been a shadow for all the sound he made. Intensely keen and vigilant as Dale was, he could not keep from swishing the grass and making an occasional rustle in the brush. Evidently the Indian did not want to lose time, but he kept cautioning Dale with an expressive backward gesture.

Nalook left the line of timber under the wall and took out into the grove. He now advanced more cautiously than ever. Dale thought this guide must have the eyes of a nighthawk. They passed a dark shack which was open in front and had a projecting roof. Two campfires were blazing a hundred yards farther on. And a lamp shone through what must have been a window of a cabin.

Presently the Indian halted. He pointed. Then Dale saw horses and men, and he heard gruff voices and the sound of flopping saddles. Some outfit had just arrived. Dale wondered if it was Reed's. If so, he had tarried some little time after getting down into the gorge.

"We go look—see," whispered Nalook in Dale's ear. The Indian seemed devoid of fear. He seemed actuated by more than friendship for Dale and gratitude to Edith Watrous. He hated someone in that horse-thief gang.

Dale followed him, growing stern and hard. He could form no idea of what to do except get the lay of the land, ascertain if possible what Reed was up to, and then go back to the head of the trail and wait for the posse. But he well realized the precarious nature of spying on these desperate men. He feared, too, that Edith Watrous was in more danger of harm than of being held for ransom.

The campfires lighted up two separate circles, both in front of the open-faced shacks. Around the farther one, men were cooking a meal. Dale smelled ham and coffee. The second fire had just been kindled and its bright blaze showed riders moving about still with chaps on, unsaddling and unpacking. Dale pierced the gloom for sight of Edith but failed to locate her.

The Indian sheered away to the right so that a cabin hid the campfires. This structure was a real log cabin of some pretensions.

Again a lamp shone through a square window. Faint streaks of light, too, came from chinks between the logs. Dale tried to see through the window, but Nalook led him at a wrong angle. Soon they reached the cabin. Dale felt the rough peeled logs. Nalook had an ear against the log wall. No sound within! Then the Indian, moving with extreme stealth, slipped very slowly along the wall until he came to one of the open chinks. Dale suppressed his eagerness. He must absolutely move without a sound. But that was easy. Thick grass grew beside the cabin. In another tense moment Dale came up with Nalook, who clutched his arm and pulled him down.

There was an aperture between the logs where the mud filling had fallen out. Dale applied his eyes to the small crack. His blood leaped at sight of a big man sitting at a table. Black-browed, scant-bearded, leonine Bill Mason! A lamp with a white globe shed a bright light. Dale saw a gun on the corner of the table, some buckskin sacks, probably containing gold, in front of Mason, and some stacks of greenbacks. An open canvas pack sat on the floor beside the table. Another pack, half-full, and surrounded by articles of clothing, added to Dale's conviction that the horse-thief leader was preparing to leave this rendezvous. The dark frown on Mason's brow appeared to cast its shadow over his strong visage.

A woman's voice, high-pitched and sweet, coming through the open door of the cabin, rang stingingly on Dale's ears.

". . . I told you . . . Keep your horsy hands off me. I can walk."

Mason started up in surprise. "A woman! Now what in hell?"

Then Edith Watrous, pale and worn, her hair disheveled and her dress so ripped that she had to hold it together, entered the cabin and fixed dark and angry eyes upon the two-faced rancher. Behind her, cool and sardonic, master of the situation, appeared Reed, blocking the door as if to keep anyone else out.

"Mr. Mason, I am Edith—Watrous," panted the girl.

"You needn't tell me that. I know you . . . What in the world are you doing here?" rejoined Mason slowly, as he arose to his commanding height. He exhibited dismay, but he was courteous.

"I've been—treated to an—outrage. I was in Halsey—visiting friends. There was a horse sale . . . I went out. I found my horse Dick—and saw other Watrous' horses in the bunch . . . I promptly told this man Reed—it was my horse. He argued with me . . . Then Hildrith came up—and that precipitated trouble. Reed put something up to Hildrith—I didn't get just what. But it looks bad. I thought he was going to kill Hildrith. But he didn't. He cursed Hildrith and said he'd see what the boss would do about it . . . They threw me on Reed's horse—made me straddle his saddle in front— and I had to endure a long ride—with my dress up to my head—my legs exposed to brush— and what was more to—to the eyes of Reed and his louts...It was terrible...I'm so perfectly furious that—that—"

She choked in her impassioned utterance.

"Miss Watrous, I don't blame you," said Mason. "Please understand this is not my doing." Then he fastened his black angry eyes upon his subordinate. "Fool! What's your game?"

"Boss, I didn't have any," returned Reed coolly. "I just saw red. It popped into my head to make off with this stuck-up Watrous woman. And here we are."

"Reed, you're lying. You've got some deep game...Jim Watrous was a friend of mine. I can't stand for such an outrage to his daughter."

"You'll have to stand it, Mason. You and I split, you know, over this last deal. It's just as I gambled would happen. You've ruined us. We're through."

"Ha! I can tell you as much."

"There was a wild-horse hunter down at Halsey—Dale Brittenham. I know about him. He's the man who trailed Ben, Alec and Steve—killed them. He's onto us. I saw that. He'll have a hundred gunners on our trail by sun up."

"Ed, that's not half of what we're up against," replied the chief gloomily. "This homesteader Rogers, with his trail to Bannock—that settled our hash. Stafford and Watrous have a big outfit after us. I heard it at Bannock. That's why I sold out. I'm leaving here as soon as I can pack."

89

"Fine. That's like you. Engineered all the jobs and let us do the stealing while you hobnobbed with the ranchers you robbed. Now you'll leave us to fight...Mason, I'm getting out too—and I'm taking the girl."

"Good God! Ed, it's bad enough to be a horse thief like this...Why man, it's madness! What for, I ask you?"

"That's my business."

"You want to make Watrous pay to get her back. He'd do it, of course. But he'd tear Montana to pieces, and hang you."

"I might take his money—later. But I confess to a weakness for the young lady ...And I'll get even with Hildrith."

"Revenge, eh? You always hated Leale. But what's he got to do with your game?"

"He's crazy in love with her. Engaged to marry her."

"He *was* engaged to me, Mr. Mason," interposed Edith scornfully. "I thought I cared for him. But I really didn't. I despise him now. I wouldn't marry him if he was the last man on earth."

"Reed, does she know?" asked Mason significantly.

"Well, she's not dumb, and I reckon she's got a hunch."

"I'll be...!" Whatever Mason's profanity was he did not give it utterance. "Hildrith! But we had plans to pull stakes and leave this country. Did he intend to marry Miss Watrous and bring her with us?...That's not conceivable."

"Boss, he cheated you. He never meant to leave."

Mason made a passionate gesture, and as if to strike deep and hard, his big eyes rolled in a fierce glare. It was plain now to the watching Dale why Reed had wanted Hildrith to face his chief.

"Where's Hildrith?" growled Mason.

"Out by the fire under guard."

"Call him in." Reed went out.

Then Edith turned wonderingly and fearfully to Mason.

"Hildrith is *your* man!" she affirmed rather than queried.

"Yes, Miss Watrous, he was."

"Then *he* is the spy, the scout—the traitor who acted as go-between for you.".

Miss Watrous, he certainly has been my right-hand man for eight years...And I'm afraid Reed and you are right about his being a traitor."

At that juncture Hildrith lunged into the cabin as if propelled viciously from behind. He was ashen-hued under his beard. Reed stamped in after him, forceful and malignant, sure of the issue. But just as Mason, after a steady look at his lieutenant, was about to address him, Edith flung herself in front of Hildrith.

"It's all told, Leale Hildrith," she cried, with a fury of passion. "Reed gave you away. Mason corroborated him ... *You* are the tool of these men. *You* were the snake in the grass. *You*, the liar who ingratiated himself into my

91

father's confidence. Made love to me! Nagged me until I was beside myself!...But your wrong to me—your betrayal of Dad—these fall before your treachery to Dale Brittenham...You let *him* take on your guilt...Oh, I see it all now. It's ghastly. That man loved you...You despicable—despicable...."

Edith broke off, unable to find further words. With tears running down her colorless cheeks, her eyes magnificent with piercing fire, she manifestly enthralled Reed with her beauty and passion. She profoundly impressed Mason and she struck deep into what manhood the stricken Hildrith had left.

"All true, Bill, I'm sorry to confess," he said, his voice steady. "I'm offering no excuse. But look at her, man...look at her! And then you'll understand."

"What's that, Miss, about Dale Brittenham?" queried Mason.

"Brittenham is a wild-horse hunter," answered Edith, catching her breath. "Hildrith befriended him once. Dale loved Hildrith...When Stafford came to see Dad—after the last raid—he accused Dale of being the spy who kept your gang posted. The go-between. He had the sheriff come to arrest Dale...Oh, I see it all now. Dale *knew* Hildrith was the traitor. He sacrificed himself for Hildrith—to pay his debt—or because he thought I loved the man. For us both!...He drew a gun on Bayne—said Stafford was right—that *he* was the horse-thief spy...then he rode away."

It was a poignant moment. No man could

have been unaffected by the girl's tragic story. Mason paced to and fro, then halted behind the table.

"Boss, that's not all," interposed Reed triumphantly. "Down at Halsey, Hildrith showed his color—and what meant most to him. Brittenham was there, as I've told you. And *he* was onto us. I saw the jig was up. I told Hildrith. I put it up to him. To declare himself. Every man there had waked up to the fact that we were horse thieves. I asked Hildrith to make his stand—for or against us. He failed us, boss."

"Reed, that was a queer thing for you to insist on," declared Mason, in stern doubt. "Hildrith's cue was the same as mine. Respictability. Could you expect him to betray himself there—before all Halsey and his sweetheart, too?"

"I knew he wouldn't. But I meant it."

"You wanted to show him up, before them all, especially her?"

"I certainly did."

"Well, you're low-down yourself, Reed, when it comes to one you hate."

"All's fair in love and war," replied the other with a flippant laugh.

The chief turned to Hildrith. "I'm not concerned with the bad blood between you and Reed. But—is he lying?"

"No. But down at Halsey I didn't understand he meant me to give myself away," replied Hildrith, with the calmness of bitter resignation. He had played a great game, for a great stake, and he had lost. Friendship, loyalty, treachery, were nothing compared to his love for this girl.

"Would you have done so if you had understood Reed?"

"No. Why should I? There was no disloyalty in that. If I'd guessed that, I'd have shot him."

"You didn't think quick and right. That'd have been your game. Too late, Hildrith. I've a hunch it's too late for all of us . . . You meant to marry Miss Watrous if she'd have you?"

"Why ask that?"

"Well, it was unnecessary . . . And you really let this Brittenham sacrifice himself for you?"

"Yes, I'd have sacrificed anyone—my own brother."

"I see. That was dirty, Leale . . . But after all these things, don't . . . You've been a faithful pard for many years. God knows a woman. . . ."

"Boss, he betrayed *you*," interrupted Reed stridently. "All the rest doesn't count. He split with you. He absolutely was not going to leave the country with you."

"I get that—hard as it is to believe," rasped Mason, and he took up the big gun from the table and deliberately cocked it.

Edith cried out low and falteringly. "Oh— don't kill him! If it was for me, spare him!"

Reed let out that sardonic laugh. "Bah! He'll deny—he'll lie with his last breath."

"That wouldn't save you, Leale—but—" Mason halted, the dark embodiment of honor among thieves.

"Hell! I deny nothing," rang out Hildrith, with something grand in his defiance. "It's all

94

true. I broke over the girl. I was through with you, Mason—you and your raids, you and your lousy sneak here—you and your low-down...."

The leveled gun boomed to cut short Hildrith's wild denunciation. Shot through the heart, he swayed a second, his distorted visage fixing, and then, with a single explosion of gasping breath, he fell backward through the door.

A heavy cloud of smoke obscured Dale's sight of the center of the cabin. As he leaned there near the window, strung like a quivering wire, he heard the thump of Mason's gun on the table. It made the gold coins jingle in their sacks. The thud of boots and hoarse shouts arose on the far side of the cabin. Then the smoke drifted away to expose Mason hunched back against the table, peering through the door into the blackness. Reed knelt on the floor where Edith had sunk in a faint.

Other members of the gang arrived outside the cabin. "Hyar! It's Hildrith. Reckon the boss croaked him."

"Mebbe Reed did it. He sure was hankerin' to."

"How air you, Chief?" called a third man, presenting a swarthy face in the lamplight.

"I'm—all right," replied Mason huskily. "Hildrith betrayed us. I bored him...Drag him away...You can divide what you find on him."

"Hey, I'm in on that," called Reed, as the swarthy man backed away from the door. "Lay hold, fellers."

Slow, labored footfalls died away. Mason opened his gun to eject the discharged shell and to replace it with one from his belt.

"She keeled over," said Reed as he lifted the girl's head.

"So I see...Sudden and raw for a tenderfoot. I'm damn glad she hated him...Did you see him feeling for his gun?"

"No. It's just as well I took that away from him on the way up. Nothing yellow about Hildrith at the finish."

"Queer what a woman can do to a man! Reed, haven't you lost your head over this one?"

"Hell yes!" exploded the other.

"Better turn her loose. She'll handicap you. This hole will be swarming with posses tomorrow."

"You're sloping tonight?"

"I am...How many horses did you sell?"

"Eighty odd. None under a hundred dollars. And we drove back the best."

"Keep it. Pay your outfit. We're square. My advice is to let this Watrous girl go, and make tracks away from here."

"Thanks...But I won't leave my tracks," returned Reed constrainedly. "She's coming too."

"Pack her out of here...Reed, I wouldn't be in your boots for a million."

"And just why, boss?"

"Women always were your weakness. Your only one. You'll hang on to the Watrous girl."

"You bet your life I will."

"Don't bet my life on it. You're gambling your own. And you'll lose it."

Reed picked up the reviving Edith and took her through the door, turning sidewise to keep from striking her head. Dale's last glimpse of his gloating expression, as he gazed down into her face, nerved him to instant and reckless action. Reed had turned to the left outside the door, which gave Dale the impression that he did not intend to carry the girl to the campfires.

Nalook touched Dale and silently indicated that he would go around his end of the cabin. Dale turned to the left. At the corner he waited to peer out. He saw a dark form cross the campfire light. Reed! He was turning away from his comrades, now engaged in a heated hubbub, no doubt over money and valuables they had found on Hildrith.

Dale had to fight his overwhelming eagerness. He stole out to follow Reed. The man made directly for the shack that Dale and Nalook had passed on their stalk to the cabin. Dale did not stop to see if the Indian followed, though he expected him to do so. Dale held himself to an absolutely noiseless stealth. The deep grass made that possible.

Edith let out a faint cry, scarcely audible. It seemed to loose springs of fire in Dale's muscles. He glided on, gaining upon the outlaw with his burden. They drew away from the vicinity of the campfires. Soon Dale grew sufficiently accustomed to the starlight to keep track of Reed. The girl was speaking incoherently. Dale would rather have had her still unconscious. She might scream and draw Reed's comrades in that direction.

Under the trees, between the bunches of scrub oak, Reed hurried. His panting breath grew quite audible. Edith was no slight burden, especially as she had begun to struggle in his arms.

"Where?...Who? Let me down," she cried, but weakly.

"Shut up, or I'll bat you one," he panted.

The low shack loomed up blacker than the shadows. A horse, tethered in the gloom, snorted at Reed's approach. Dale, now only a few paces behind the outlaw, gathered all his forces for a spring.

"Let me go...Let me go...I'll scream—"

"Shut up, I tell you. If you scream I'll choke you. If you fight, I'll beat you."

"But, Reed—for God's sake!...You're not drunk. You must be mad—if you mean...."

"Girl, I didn't know what—I meant—when I grabbed you down there," he panted, passionately, "but I know now...I'm taking you away—Edith Watrous—out of Montana ...But tonight, by heaven!"

Dale closed in swiftly and silently. With relentless strength he crushed a strangling hold around Reed's neck. The man snorted as his head went back. The girl dropped with a sudden gasp. Then Dale, the fingers of his left hand buried in Reed's throat, released his right hand to grasp his gun. He did not dare to shoot, but he swung the weapon to try to stun

Reed. He succeeded in landing only a glancing blow.

"Aggh!" gasped Reed, and for an instant his body appeared to sink.

Dale tried to strike again. Because of Reed's sudden grip on his arm he could not exert enough power. The gun stuck. Dale felt it catch in the man's coat. Reed let out a strangled yell, which Dale succeeded in choking off again.

Suddenly the outlaw let go Dale's right hand and reached for his gun. He got to it, but could not draw, due to Dale's constricting arm. Dale pressed with all his might. They staggered, swayed bound together as with bands of steel. Dale saw that if his hold loosened on either Reed's throat or gun hand, the issue would be terribly perilous. Reed was the larger and more powerful, though now at a disadvantage. Dale hung on like the grim death he meant to mete out to that man.

Suddenly, with a tremendous surge, Reed broke Dale's hold and bent him back. Then Dale saw he would be forced to shoot. But even as he struggled with the gun, Reed, quick as a cat, intercepted it, and with irresistible strength turned the weapon away while he drew his own. Dale was swift to grasp that with his left hand. A terrific struggle ensued, during which the grim and silent combatants both lost hold of their guns.

Reed succeeded in drawing a knife, which he swung aloft. Dale caught his wrist and jerked down on it with such tremendous force that he caused the outlaw to stab himself in the side. Then Dale grappled him round the waist, pinning both arms to Reed's sides, so that he was unable to withdraw the knife. Not only that, but soon Dale's inexorable pressure sank the blade in to the hilt. A horrible panting sound escaped Reed's lips.

Any moment Nalook might come to end this desperate struggle. The knife stuck in Reed's side, clear to the hilt. Dale had the thought that he must hold on until Reed collapsed. Then he would have to run with Edith and try to get up the trail. He could not hope to find the horses in that gloomy shadow.

Reed grew stronger in his frenzy. He whirled so irresistibly that he partly broke Dale's hold. They plunged down, with Dale on the top and Reed under him. Dale had his wind almost shut off. Another moment... but Reed rolled like a bear. Dale, now underneath, wound his left arm around Reed. Over and over they rolled, against the cabin, back against a tree, and then over a bank. The shock broke both Dale's holds. Reed essayed to yell, but only a hoarse sound came forth. Suddenly he had weakened. Dale beat at him with his right fist. Then he reached for the knife in Reed's side, found the shaft, and wrenched so violently that he cracked Reed's ribs. The man suddenly relaxed. Dale tore the knife out and buried it in Reed's breast.

That ended the fight. Reed sank shudderingly into a limp state. Dale slowly got up, drawing the knife with him. He had sustained no injury that he could ascertain at the moment. He was wet with sweat or blood, probably both. He slipped the knife in his belt, and untied his scarf to wipe his hands and face. Then he climbed up the bank, expecting to see Edith's white blouse in the darkness.

But he did not see it. Nor was Nalook there. He called low. No answer! He began to search around on the ground. He found his gun. Then he went into the shack. Edith was gone and Nalook had not come. Possibly he might have come while the fight was going on down over the bank and, seeing the chance to save Edith, had made off with her to the horses.

Dale listened. The crickets were in loud voice. He could see the campfires, and heard nothing except the thud of hoofs. They seemed fairly close. He retraced his steps back to the shack. Reed's horse was gone. Dale strove for control over his whirling thoughts. He feared that Edith, in her terror, had run off at random, to be captured again by some of the outlaws. After a moment's consideration, he dismissed that as untenable. She had fled, unquestionably, but without a cry, which augured well. Dalle searched the black rim for the notch that marked the trail. Then he set off.

Reaching the belt of brush under the rim he followed it until he came to an opening he thought he recognized. A stamp of hoofs electrified him. He hurried toward it and presently emerged into a glade less gloomy. First his keen sight distinguished Edith's white blouse. She was either sitting or lying on the ground. Then he saw the horses. As he hurried forward, Nalook met him.

"Nalook! Is she all right?" he whispered eagerly.

"All same okay. No hurt."

"What'd you do?"

"Me foller. See girl run. Me ketch."

"Go back to that shack and search Reed. He must have a lot of money on him ... We rolled over a bank."

"Ugh!" The Indian glided away.

Dale went on to find Edith sitting propped against a stone. He could not distinguish her features but her posture was eloquent of spent force.

"Edith," he called gently.

"Oh, Dale! ... Are you—?"

"I'm all right," he replied hastily.

"You—you killed him?"

"Of course. I had to. Are you hurt?"

"Only bruised. That ride! ... Then he handled me—Oh, the brute! I'm glad you killed ... I saw you bend him back—hit him. I knew you. But it was awful ... And seeing Leale murdered—so suddenly—right before my eyes—that was worse."

"Put all that out of your mind ... Let me help you up. We can't stay here long. Your hands are like ice," he whispered as he got her up.

"I'm freezing—to death," she replied. "This thin waist. I left my coat in the buckboard."

"Here. Slip into mine." Dale helped her into his coat, and then began to rub her cold hands between his.

"Dale, I wasn't afraid of Reed—at first. I scorned him. I saw how his men liked that. I kept telling him that you would kill him for this outrage to me. That if *you* didn't Dad would hang him. But there in Mason's cabin—there I realized my danger... You must have been close."

"Yes. Nalook and I watched between the logs. I saw it all. But I tell you to forget it."

"Oh, will I ever?... Dale, you saved me from God only knows what," she whispered, and putting her arms around his neck, she leaned upon his breast, and looked up. Out of her pale face great midnight eyes that reflected the starlight transfixed him with their mystery and passion. "You liar. You fool!" she went on, her soft voice belying the hard words. "You poor misguided man! To dishonor your name for Hildrith's sake! To tell Stafford he was right! To let Dad hear you say you were a horse thief! Oh! I shall never forgive you."

"My dear. I did it—for Leale—and perhaps more for your sake," replied Dale unsteadily. "I thought you loved him. That there was chance to reform. He would have done it, too, if—"

"I don't care what he would have done. I imagined I loved him. But I didn't. I was a vain, silly, headstrong girl. And I was influenced. I don't believe I ever could have married him—after you brought back my horses. I didn't realize then. But when I kissed you—Oh, Dale! Something tore through my heart. I know now. It was love. Even then, what I needed was this horrible experience. It has awakened me... Oh, Dale, if I loved you then, what do you think it is now?"

"I can't think—dearest," whispered Dale huskily, as he drew her closer, and bent over to lay his face against her hair. "Only, if you're not out of your mind, I'm the luckiest man thet ever breathed."

"Dale, I'm distraught, yes, and my heart is bursting. But I know I love you...love you. Love you! Oh, with all my mind and soul!"

Dale's heart throbbed in tumultuous exaltation, and he stood holding her with an intensely vivid sense of the place and moment. The ragged rim loomed above them, dark and forbidding, as if to warn; the incessant chirp of crickets, the murmur of running water, the rustle of the wind in the brush, proved that he was alive and awake, living the most poignant moment of his life.

Then Nalook glided silently into the glade. Dale released Edith, and stepped back to meet the Indian. Nalook thrust into his hands a heavy bundle tied up in a scarf.

"Me keep gun." he said, and bent over his saddle.

"What'll we do, Nalook?" asked Dale.

"Me stay—watch trail. You take girl Halsey."

"Dale, I couldn't ride it. I'm exhausted. I can hardly stand," interposed Edith.

"Reckon I'd get lost in the dark," returned Dale thoughtfully. "I've a better plan. There's a homesteader in this valley. Man named Rogers. I knew him over in the mountains. An' I ran across his cabin a day or so ago. It's not far. I'll take you there. Then tomorrow I'll go with you to Bannock, or send you with him."

"Send me!"

"Yes. I've got to be here. Strickland agreed to send a posse after me in half an hour—an' later a big outfit of cowboys."

"But you've rescued me. Need you stay? Nalook can guide these men."

"I reckon I want to help clean out these horse thieves."

"Bayne is on your trail with a posse."

"Probably he's with Stafford's outfit."

"That won't clear you of Stafford's accusation."

"No. But Strickland an' his outfit will clear me. I must be here when thet fight comes off. If it comes. You heard Mason say he was leavin' tonight. I reckon they'll all get out pronto."

"Dale! you—you might get shot—or even ...Oh, these are wicked, hard men!" exclaimed Edith, as she fastened persuasive hands on his coatless arms.

"Thet's the chance I must run to clear my name, Edith," he rejoined gravely.

"You took a fearful chance with Reed."

"Yes. But he had you in his power."

"My life and more were at stake then," she said earnestly. "It's still my love and my happiness."

"Edith, I'll have Nalook beside me an' we'll fight like Indians. I swear I'll come out of it alive."

"The—go ahead—anyway..." she whispered almost inaudibly, and let her nerveless hands drop from him.

"Nalook, you watch the trail," ordered Dale.

"Stop any man climbing out. When Strickland's posse comes, hold them till the cowboys get here. If I hear shots this way, I'll come pronto."

The Indian grunted and, taking up his rifle, stole away. Dale untied and led his horse up to where his saddle lay. Soon he had him saddled and bridled. Then he put on his spurs, which the Indian had remembered to get.

"Come," said Dale, reaching for Edith. When he lifted her, it came home to him why Reed had not found it easy to carry her.

"That's comfortable, if I can stay on," she said, settling herself.

"Hoof, old boy," whispered Dale to his horse. "No actin' up. This'll be the most precious load you ever carried."

Then Dale, rifle in hand, took the bridle and led the horse out into the open. The lake gleamed like a black star-lit mirror. Turning to the right, Dale slowly chose the ground and walked a hundred steps or more before he halted to listen. He went on and soon crossed the trail. Beyond that he breathed easier, and did not stop again until he had half circled the lake. He saw lights across the water up among the trees, but heard no alarming sound.

"How're you ridin'?" he whispered to Edith.

"I can stick on if it's not too far."

"Half a mile more."

As he proceeded, less fearful of being heard, he began to calculate about where he should look for Rogers' canyon. He had carefully marked it almost halfway between the two lakes and directly across from the highest point of the rim. When Dale got abreast of this, he headed to the right and was soon under the west wall. Then despite the timber on the rim and the shadowed background, he located a gap which he made certain marked the canyon.

But he could not find any trail leading into it. Therefore he began to work cautiously through the thickets. The gurgle and splash of running water guided him. It was so pitch black that he had to feel his way. The watercourse turned out to be rocky and he abandoned that. When he began to fear he was headed wrong a dark tunnel led him out into the open canyon. He went on and turned a corner to catch the gleam of a light. Then he rejoiced at his good fortune. In a few minutes more he arrived at the cabin. The door was open. Dale heard voices.

"Hey, Rogers, are you home?" he called.

An exclamation and thud of bootless feet attested to the homesteader's presence. The next instant he appeared in the door.

"Who's thar?"

"Brittenham," replied Dale, and lifting Edith off the saddle, he carried her up on the porch into the light. Rogers came out in amazement. His wife cried from the door, "For the land's sake!"

"Wal, a gurl! Aw, don't say she's hurt," burst out the homesteader.

"You bet it's a girl. An' thank heaven she's sound! Jim Watrous's daughter, Rogers. She was kidnapped by Reed at the Halsey horse sale. Thet happened this afternoon. I just got her back. Now, Mrs. Rogers, will you take her in for tonight? Hide her someplace."

"That I will. She can sleep in the loft...Come in, my dear child. You're white as a sheet."

"Thank you. I've had enough to make me green," replied Edith, limping into the cabin.

Dale led Rogers out of earshot. "Hell will bust loose here about tomorrow," he said, and briefly told about the several posses en route for the horse thieves' stronghold, and the events relating to the capture and rescue of Edith.

"By gad! Thet's all good," ejaculated the homesteader. "But it's not so good—all of us hyar if they have a big fight."

"Maybe the gang will slope. Mason is leavin'. I heard him tell Reed. An' Reed meant to take the girl. I don't know about the rest of them."

"Wal, these fellers ain't likely to rustle in the dark. They've been too secure. An' they figger they can't be surprised at night."

"If Mason leaves by the lower trail, he'll get shot. My Indian pard is watchin' there."

"Gosh, I hope he tries it."

"Mason had his table loaded with bags of coin an' stacks of bills. We sure ought to get thet an' pay back the people he's robbed."

"It's a good bet Mason won't take the upper trail...Brittenham, you look fagged. Better have some grub an' drink. An' sleep a little."

"Sure. But I'm a bloody mess, an' don't want the women to see me. Fetch me something out here."

Later Dale and Rogers walked down to the valley. They did not see any lights or hear any sounds. Both ends of the gorge, where the trails led up, were dark and silent. They returned, and Dale lay down on the porch on some sheepskins. He did not expect to sleep. His mind was too full. Only the imminence of a battle could have kept his mind off the wondrous and incomprehensible fact of Edith's avowal. After pondering over the facts and probabilities Dale decided a fight was inevitable. Mason and Reed had both impressed him as men at the end of their ropes. The others would, no doubt, leave, though not so hurriedly, and most probably would be met on the way out.

Long after Rogers' cabin was dark and its inmates wrapped in slumber, Dale lay awake, listening, thinking, revolving plans to get Edith safely away and still not seem to shirk his share of the fight. But at last, worn out by strenuous activity and undue call on his emotions, Dale fell asleep.

A step on the porch aroused him. It was broad daylight. Rogers was coming in with an armload of firewood.

"All serene, Brittenham," he said, with satisfaction.

"Good. I'll wash an' slip down to get a look at the valley."

"Wal, I'd say if these outfits of cowboys was on hand, they'd be down long ago."

"Me too." Dale did not go clear out into the gateway of the valley. He climbed a small hill and surveyed the gorge from the lookout.

Sweeping the gray-green valley with eager gaze, he failed to see a moving object. Both upper and lower ends of the gorge appeared as vacant as they were silent. But at length his attention quickened sharply to columns of blue smoke rising above the timber up from the lower lake. He watched for a good hour. The sun rose over the gap at the east rim. Concluding that posses and cowboys had yet to arrive, Dale descended the bluff and retraced his steps toward the cabin.

He considered sending Edith out in charge of Rogers, to conduct her as far as Bannock. This idea he at once conveyed to Rogers.

"Don't think much of it," returned the homesteader forcibly. "Better hide her an' my family in a cave. I know where they'll be safe until this fracas is over."

"Well! I reckon thet is better."

"Come in an' eat. Then we'll go scoutin'. An' if we see any riders, we'll rustle back to hide the women an' kids."

Dale had about finished a substantial breakfast when he thought he heard a horse neigh somewhere in the distance. He ran out on the porch and was suddenly shocked to a standstill. Scarcely ten paces out stood a man with leveled rifle.

"Hands up, Britt," he ordered, with a hissing breath. Two other men, just behind him, leaped forward to present guns, and one of them yelled, "Hyar he is, Bayne."

"Rustle! Up with 'em!"

Then Dale, realizing the cold, bitter fact of

110

an unlooked-for situation, shot up his arms just as Rogers came stamping out.

"What the hell? *Who....*"

Six or eight more men, guns in hands, appeared at the right, led by the red-faced sheriff of Salmon. He was bursting with importance and vicious triumph. Dale surveyed the advancing group, among whom he recognized old enemies, and then his gaze flashed back to the first man with the leveled rifle. This was none other than Pickens, a crooked, young horse trader who had all the reason in the world to gloat over rounding up Dale in this way.

"Guess I didn't have a hunch up thar, fellers, when we crossed this trail," declared Bayne in loud voice. "Guess I didn't measure his hoss tracks down at Watrous's for nothin'!"

"Bayne, you got the drop," spoke up Dale cooly, "and I'm not fool enough to draw in the face of thet."

"You did draw on me once, though, didn't you, wild-hoss hunter?" called Bayne derisively.

"Yes."

"An' you told Stafford he was right, didn't you?"

"Yes, but—"

"No buts. You admitted you was a hoss thief, didn't you?"

"Rogers here can explain thet, if you won't listen to me."

"Wal, Brittenham, your homesteadin' pard

can explain thet after we hang you!"

Rogers stalked off the porch in the very face of the menacing guns and confronted Bayne in angry expostulation.

"See here, Mister Bayne, you're on the wrong track."

"We want no advice from you," shouted Bayne. "An' you'd better look out or we'll give you the same dose."

"Boss, he's shore to be one of this hoss-thief gang," spoke up a lean, weathered member of the posse.

"My name's Rogers. I'm a homesteader. I have a wife an' two children. There are men in Bannock who'll vouch for my honesty," protested Rogers.

"Reckon so. But they ain't here. You stay out of this...Hold him up, men."

Two of them prodded the homesteader with cocked rifles, a reckless and brutal act that would have made the bravest man turn gray. Rogers put up shaking hands.

"Friend Rogers, don't interfere," warned Dale, who had grasped the deadly nature of Bayne's procedure. The sheriff believed Dale was one of the mysterious band of thieves that had been harassing the ranchers of Salmon River Valley for a long time. It had galled him, no doubt, to fail to bring a single thief to justice. Added to that was animosity toward Dale and a mean leaning to exercise his office. He wanted no trial. He would brook no opposition. Dale stood there a self-confessed criminal.

"Rope Brittenham," ordered Bayne. "Tie

his hands behind his back. Bore him if he as much as winks."

Two of the posse dragged Dale off the porch, and in a moment had bound him securely. Then Dale realized too late that he should have leaped while he was free to snatch a gun from one of his captors, and fought it out. He had not taken seriously Bayne's threat to hang him. But he saw now that unless a miracle came to pass, he was doomed. The thought was so appalling that it clamped him momentarily in an icy terror. Edith was at the back of that emotion. He had faced death before without flinching, but to be hanged while Edith was there, possibly a witness— that would be too horrible. Yet he read it in the hard visages of Bayne and his men. By a tremendous effort he succeeded in getting hold of himself.

"Bayne, this job is not law," he expostulated. "It's revenge. When my innocence is proved, you'll be in a tight fix."

"Innocence! Hell man, didn't you confess your guilt?" ejaculated Bayne. "Stafford heard you, same as Watrous an' his friends."

"All the same, thet was a lie."

"Aw, it was? My Gawd, man, but you take chances with your life! An' what'd you lie for?"

"I lied for Edith Watrous."

Bayne stared incredulously and then he guffawed. He turned to his men.

"Reckon we better shet off his wind. The man's plumb loco."

From behind Dale a noose, thrown by a

lanky cowboy, sailed and widened to encircle his head, and to be drawn tight. The hard knot came just under Dale's chin and shut off the hoarse cry that formed involuntarily.

"Over thet limb, fellers," called out Bayne briskly, pointing to a spreading branch of a pinon tree some few yards farther out. Dale was dragged under it. The loose end of the rope was thrown over the branch, to fall into eager hands.

"Dirty bisness, Bayne, you—!" shouted Rogers, shaken by horror and wrath. "So help me Gawd, you'll rue it!"

Bayne leered malignantly, plainly in the grip of passion too strong for reason.

"Thar's five thousand dollars' reward wrapped up in this wild-hoss hunter's hide an' I ain't takin' any chance of losin' it."

Dale forced a strangled utterance. "Bayne—I'll double thet if you'll arrest me...give...fair trial."

"Haw! Haw! Wal, listen to our ragged hoss thief talk big money."

"Boss, he aint got two bits...We're wastin' time."

"Swing him, fellers!"

Four or five men stretched the rope and had lifted Dale to his toes when a piercing shriek from the cabin startled them so violently that they let him down again. Edith Watrous came flying out, half dressed, her hair down, her face blanched. Her white blouse fluttered in her hand as she ran, bare-foot, across the grass.

"Merciful heaven! Dale! That rope!" she

screamed, and as the shock of realization came, she dropped her blouse to the ground and stood stricken before the staring men, her bare round arms and lovely shoulders shining white in the sunlight. Her eyes darkened, dilated, enlarged as her consciousness grasped the significance here, and then fixed in terror.

Dale's ghastly sense of death faded. This girl would save him. A dozen Baynes could not contend with Edith Watrous, once she was roused.

"Edith, they were about—to hang me."

"*Hang you?*" she cried, suddenly galvanized. "These men?...*Bayne?*"

Leaping red blood burned out the pallor of her face. It swept away in a wave, leaving her whiter than before, and with eyes like coals of living fire.

"Miss Watrous. What you—doin' here?" queried Bayne, halting, confused by this apparition.

"I'm here—not quite too late," she replied, as if to herself, and a ring of certainty in her voice followed hard on the tremulous evidence of her thought.

"Kinda queer—meetin' you up here in this outlaw's den," went on Bayne with a nervous cough.

"Bayne...I remember," she said ponderingly, ignoring his statement. "The gossip linking Dale's name with this horse-thief outfit...Stafford!...Your intent to arrest Dale!...His drawing on you! His strange acceptance of Stafford's accusation!"

"Nothin' strange about thet, Miss," rejoined Bayne brusquely. "Brittenham was caught in a trap. An' like a wolf he bit back."

"That confession had to do with me, Mister Bayne" she retorted.

"So he said. But I ain't disregardin' same."

"You are not arresting him," she asserted swiftly.

"Nope, I ain't."

"But didn't you let him explain?" she queried.

"I didn't want no cock-an'-bull explainin' from him or this doubtful pard of his here, Rogers...I'll just hang Brittenham an' let Rogers talk afterwards. Reckon he'll not have much to say then."

"So, that's your plan, you miserable, thick-headed skunk of a sheriff?" she exclaimed in lashing scorn. She swept her flaming eyes from Bayne to his posse, all of whom appeared uneasy over this interruption. "Pickens! ...Hall...Jason...Pike! And some more hard nuts from Salmon. Why, if you were honest yourself, you'd arrest them. My father could put Pickens in jail...Bayne, your crew of a posse reflects suspiciously on you."

"Wal, I ain't carin' for what you think. It's plain to me you've took powerful with this hoss thief an' I reckon thet reflects suspicions on you, Miss," rejoined Bayne, galled to recimination.

A scarlet blush wiped out the whiteness of Edith's neck and face. She burned with shame and fury. That seemed to remind her of herself, of her half-dressed state, and she bent to pick up her blouse. When she rose to slip her arms through the garment, she was pale again. She forgot to button it.

"You dare not hang Brittenham."

"Wal, lady, I just do," he declared, but he was weakening somehow.

"You shall not!"

"Better go indoors, Miss. It ain't pleasant to see a man hang an' kick an' swell an' grow black in the face."

Bayne had no conception of the passion and courage of a woman. He blundered into the very speeches that made Edith a lioness.

"Take that rope off his neck," she commanded, as a queen might have to slaves.

The members of the posse shifted from one foot to the other, and betrayed that they would have looked to their leader had they been able to remove their fascinated gaze from this girl. Pickens, the nearest to her, moved back a step, holding his rifle muzzle up. The freckles stood out awkwardly on his dirty white face.

"Give me that rifle," she cried hotly, and she leaped to snatch at it. Pickens held on, his visage a study in consternation and alarm. Edith let go with one hand and struck him a staggering blow with her fist. Then she fought him for the weapon. Bang! It belched fire and smoke up into the tree. She jerked it away from him and, leaping back, she worked the lever with a swift precision that proved her familiarity with firearms. Without aiming she shot at Pickens' feet. Dale saw the bullet strike up dust between them. Pickens leaped with a wild yell and fled.

117

Edith whirled upon Bayne. She was magnificent in her rage. Such a thing as fear of these men was as far from her as if she had never experienced such an emotion. Again she worked the action of the rifle. She held it low at Bayne and pulled the trigger. Bang! The bullet sped between his legs, and burned the left one, which flinched as the man called, "Hyar! Stop thet, you fool woman. You'll kill somebody!"

"Bayne, I'll kill *you*, if you try to hang Brittenham," she replied, her voice ringing high-keyed but level and cold. "Take that noose off his neck!"

The frightened sheriff made haste to comply.

"Now untie him!"

"Help me hyar—somebody," snarled Bayne, turning Dale around to tear at the rope. "My Gawd, what's this range comin' to when wild women bust loose...? The luck! We can't shoot her! We can't rope Jim Watrous's girl!"

"Boss, I reckon it may be jist as well," replied the lean gray man who was helping him, "cause it wasn't regular."

"You men! Put away your guns," ordered Edith. "I wouldn't hesitate to shoot any one of you... Now listen, all of you... Brittenham is no horse thief. He is a man who sacrificed his name—his honor for his friend—and because he thought I loved that friend. Leale Hildrith! *He* was the treacherous spy—the go-between, the liar who deceived my father and me. Dale took his guilt. I never believed it. I followed Dale to Halsey. Hildrith followed me. There

118

we found Ed Reed and his outfit selling Watrous horses. I recognized my own horse, Dick, and I accused Reed. He betrayed Hildrith right there and kidnaped us both, and rode to his hole... We got here last night. Reed took me before Bill Mason. Big Bill, who is leader of this band. They sent for Hildrith. And Mason shot him. Reed made off with me, intending to leave. But Dale had trailed us, and he killed Reed. Then he fetched me here to this cabin... You have my word. I swear this is the truth."

"Wal, I'll be!" ejaculated Bayne, who had grown so obsessed by Edith's story that he had forgotten to untie Dale.

"Boss! Hosses comin' hell bent!" shouted one of Bayne's men, running in.

"Whar?"

A ringing trample of swift hoofs on the hard trail drowned further shouts. Dale saw a line of riders sweep round the corner and race down upon the cabin. They began to shoot into Bayne's posse. There were six riders, all shooting as hard as they were riding, and some of them had two guns leveled. Hoarse yells rose about the banging volley of shots.

The horsemen sped on past, still shooting. Bullets thudded into the cabin. The riders vanished in a cloud of dust and the clatter of hoofs died away.

Dale frantically unwound the rope which Bayne had suddenly let go during the onslaught of riders. Freeing himself, Dale leaped to Edith who had dropped the rifle and stood unsteadily, her eyes wild.

"Did they hit you?" gasped Dale, seizing her.

Rogers rushed up to join them, holding a hand to a bloody shoulder. "Some of Mason's outfit," he boomed, and he gazed around with rolling eyes. Pickens lay dead, his bloody head against the tree. Bayne had been shot through the middle. A spreading splotch of red on his shirt under his clutching hands attested to a mortal wound. Three other men lay either groaning or cursing. That left four apparently unscratched, only one of whom, a lean oldish man, showed any inclination to help his comrades.

"Lemme see how bad you're hit," he was growling over one of them.

"Aw, it ain't bad, but it hurts like hell."

"Edith, come, I'll take you in," said Dale, putting his arm around the weakening girl.

"Britt, I've a better idee," put in Rogers. "I'll take her an' my family to the cave where they'll be safe."

"Good! Thet outfit must have been chased."

"We'd have heard shots. I reckon they were rustlin' away and jest piled into us."

The two reached the cabin, where Dale said, "Brace up, Edith. It sure was tough. It'll be all right now."

"Oh, I'm sick," she whispered, as she leaned against him.

Rogers went in, calling to his wife. Dale heard him rummaging around. Soon he appeared in the door and handed a tin box and a bundle of linen to Dale.

"Those hombres out there can take care of their own wounded."

Dale pressed Edith's limp hand and begged earnestly, "Don't weaken now, dear. Good Lord, how wonderful an' terrible you were! Edith, I'll bear a charmed life after this . . . Go with Rogers."

"I'll be all right," she replied with a pale smile. "Go—do what's best—but don't stay long away from me."

Hurrying out, Dale found all save one of the wounded on their feet.

"Wal, thet's decent of you," said the lean, hawk-faced man, as he received the bandages and medicine from Dale. "Bayne jist croaked an' he can stay croaked right there for all I care. I'm sorry he made the mistake takin' you for a hoss thief."

"He paid for it," rejoined Dale grimly. "You must bury him and Pickens. I'll fetch you some tools. But move them away from here."

Dale searched around until he found a spade and mattock, which he brought back. Meanwhile the spokesman of Bayne's posse and Jason Pike had about concluded a hasty binding of the injured men.

"Brittenham, we come down this trail from Bannock. Are there any other ways to get in an' out of this hole?"

"Look here," replied Dale, and squatted down to draw an oval in the dust. "This represents the valley. It runs almost directly north an' south. There's a trail at each end. This trail of Rogers' leads out of here, almost due west, an' leads to Bannock. There might be, an' very probably is, another trail on the east side, perhaps back of Mason's camp. But Nalook didn't tell me there was."

"Thet outfit who rid by here to smoke us up—they must have been chased or at least scared."

"Chased, I figure that, though no cowboys appear to be comin' along. You know Stafford an' Watrous were sendin' a big outfit of cowboys up from Salmon. They'll come down the south trail. An' I'm responsible for two more, raised by a rancher named Strickland over at Halsey. They are due an' they'll come in at the lower end of the hole. The north end."

"Wal, I'd like to be in on thet round-up. What say, Jason?"

"Hell, yes. But Tom, you'd better send Jerry an' hike out with our cripples. They'd just handicap us."

"Reckon so. Now let's rustle to put these stiffs under the sod an' the dew. Strip them of valuables. Funny about Bayne. He was sure rarin' to spend that five thousand Stafford offered for Brittenham alive or dead."

"Bayne had some faults. Hyar, fellars, give us a hand."

"I'll rustle my horse," said Dale, and strode off. He had left Hoofs to graze at will, but the sturdy bay was nowhere in sight. Finally Dale found him in Rogers' corral with two other horses. He led Hoofs back to the cabin, and was saddling him when he saw Rogers crossing the brook into the open. Evidently he had taken the women and children somewhere in that direction. Dale's keen eye approved of the dense thicket of brush and trees leading up to a great wall of cliffs and caverns and splintered sections. They would be safely hidden in there.

Then Dale remembered his gun, which Pickens had taken from him. He found it under the tree with the weapons, belts and spurs of the slain men. Dale took up the carbine that Pickens had left, and which Edith had wrenched out of his hands. He decided he would like to keep it, and carried it to the cabin.

Tom and Pike, with the third man, returned from their gruesome task somewhere below. The next move was to send the four cripples, one of whom lurched in his saddle, up the trail to Bannock with their escort.

When Dale turned from a dubious gaze after them, he sighted Nalook riding up from the valley. The Indian was approaching warily. Dale hallooed and strode out to meet him.

"Me come slow—look see."

"Nalook, those tracks were made by six of Mason's outfit who rode through, hell bent for election."

"Me hear shots."

"They killed Bayne an' one of his posse, an' crippled four more."

"Ugh! Bayne jail Injun no more!" Nalook ejaculated with satisfaction.

"I shouldn't smile. Nalook, what's doin' down in the hole?"

"Ten paleface, three my people come sunup. No cowboy."

"Well! Thet's odd, Strickland guaranteed a big outfit. I wonder...No sign of Stafford's cowboys on the other trail?"

"Me look long, no come."

"Where's thet outfit from Halsey?"

The Indian indicated by gesture that he had detained these men at the rim.

"You watched the trail all night?"

Nalook nodded, and his inscrutable eyes directed Dale's to the back of his saddle. A dark coat of heavy material, and evidently covering a bundle, had been bound behind the cantle. Dale put a curious hand on the coat. He felt something hard inside, and that caused him to note how securely the coat had been tied on. Suddenly a dark red spot gave him a shock. Blood! He touched it to find it glazed over and dry. Dale looked into the bronzed visage and somber eyes of the Indian with a cold sense of certainty.

"Mason?"

The Indian nodded. "Me watch long. Big Bill he come. Two paleface foller. Top trail. Me watch. Big powwow. They want gold. Mason no give. Cuss like hell. They shoot. Me kill um."

"Nalook, you just beat hell!" ejaculated Dale, at once thrilled and overcome at the singular way things were working out. He had not forgotten the sacks of gold and pile of green backs on Mason's table. To let the robber chief make off with that had been no easy surrender.

"Me beat hoss thief," replied the Indian,

taking Dale literally. "Big Bill no good. He take Palouse girl away."

"Aha! So thet's why you've been so soft and gentle with these horse thieves.... Nalook, I don't want anyone, not even Rogers, to see this coat an' what's in it."

"Me savvy. Where hide?"

"Go to the barn. Hide it in the loft under the hay."

Nalook rode on by the cabin. Dale sat down on the porch to wait for his return and the others. He found himself trembling with the significance of the moment. He had possession of a large amount of money, probably more than enough to reimburse all the ranchers from whom cattle and horses had been stolen. Moreover, the losses of any poor ranchers over on the Palouse range would have to be made good. That, however, could hardly make much of a hole in the fortune Mason had no doubt been accumulating for years.

The Indian came back from the barn, leading his horse. He sat down beside Dale and laid a heavy hand on his arm.

"No look! Me see man watchin' on the rock," he said.

Nalook let go of Dale and curved a thumb that indicated a bare point on the west rim, in fact the only place for a lookout on that side, and the one from which he had planned to get Rogers' signal. On the moment Rogers returned.

"Rogers, stand pat now," said Dale. "The

Indian sighted someone watchin' us. From the bare point you know, where I was to come for our signal."

"Wal, thet ain't so good," growled the homesteader with concern. "Must be them cusses who busted through here, shootin'. By thunder, I'd like to get a crack at the feller who gave me this cut in the shoulder."

"I forgot Rogers. Is it serious?"

"Not at all. But it's sore an' makes me sore. I was fool enough to show it to my wife. But I couldn't tie it up myself. Blood always sickens wimmen."

"What do?" asked the Indian.

"We won't let on we know we're bein' watched...Rogers, could any scout on thet point see where you took your wife an' Edith?"

"I reckon not. Fact is, I'm sure not."

"Well, you stay here. It's reasonable to figure these horse thieves won't come back. An' if any others came out of the valley, they'll be stretchin' leather. You keep hid. I'll take Nalook an' these men, an' see what's up out there."

"Couldn't do no better. But you want to come back by dark, 'cause thet girl begged me to tell you," replied Rogers, earnestly. "Gosh, I never saw such eyes in a human's face. You be careful, Britt. Thet girl is jist livin' for you."

"Rogers, I'm liable to be so careful thet I'll be yellow," rejoined Dale soberly.

Soon Dale was jogging down the trail at the head of the quartet. In the brush cover at the outlet of the canyon they had to ride single file. Once out in the valley Nalook was the first to call attention to horses scattered here and there all over the green. They evidently had broken out of the pasture or had been freed. Dale viewed them and calculated their number with satisfaction. Not a rider in sight!

Dale led a brisk trot. It did not take long to reach the lower trail. Here he sent Nalook up to fetch down the ten white men and four Indians that Strickland had been able to get together. After keenly surveying the valley Dale voiced his surprise to Tom and Jason.

"Queer all right," agreed the older man. "Kinda feels like a lull before the storm."

"I wonder what happened to Stafford's outfit. They've had hours more time than needed. They've missed the trail." .

The Indian was clever. He sent the men down on foot, some distance apart. They made little noise and raised scarcely any dust. Dale looked this posse over keenly. They appeared to be mostly miners: rough, bearded, matured men. There were, however, several cowboys, one of whom Dale had seen at the horse sale. The last two to descend the trail proved to be Strickland with the Indian.

"By jove, you, Strickland!" ejaculated Dale, in surprise.

"I couldn't keep out of it, Brittenham," returned the rancher dryly. "This sort of thing is my meat. Besides, I'm pretty curious and sore."

"How about your cowboys?"

"I'm sure I can't understand why those outfits haven't shown up. But I didn't send for my own. I've only a few now and they're out on the range. Sanborn and Drew were to send theirs, with an outfit from the Circle Bar. Damn strange! This is stern range business that concerns the whole range."

"Maybe not so strange. If they were friends of Mason."

"Thick as hops!" exclaimed Strickland with a snort.

"We'll go slow an' wait for Stafford's cowboys," decided Dale ponderingly.

"Hoss thieves all get away mebbe," interposed Nalook, plainly, not liking this idea of waiting.

"All right, Nalook. What's your advice?"

"Crawl like Injun," he replied, and spread wide his fingers. "Mebbe soon shoot heap much."

"Strickland, this Indian is simply great. We'll be wise to listen to him. Take your men an' follow him. Cowboy, you hide here at the foot of the trail an' give the alarm if any riders come down. We've reason to believe some of the gang are scoutin' along this west rim. I'll slip up on top an' have a look at Mason's camp."

Drawing his rifle from its saddle sheath, Dale removed his coat and spurs. Nalook was already leading his horse into the brush, and the Indians followed him. Strickland, with a caustic word of warning to Dale, waved his men after the Indian.

"Come with me. Throw your chaps an' spurs, cowboy," advised Dale, and addressed himself to the steep trail. Soon the long-legged cowboy caught up with him, but did not speak until they reached the rim. Dale observed that he also carried a rifle and had the look of a man who could use it.

"Brittenham, if I see any sneakin' along the rim, shall I smoke 'em up?" he queried.

"You bet, unless they're cowboys."

"Wal, I shore know thet breed."

They parted. Dale stole into the evergreens, walking on his toes. He wound in and out, keeping as close to the rim as possible, and did not halt until he had covered several hundred yards. Then he listened and tried to peer over the rim. But he heard nothing and could see only the far part of the valley. Another quarter of a mile would put him where he could view Mason's camp. But he had not gone quite so far when a thud of hoofs on soft ground brought him up tight-skinned and cold. A horse was approaching at some little distance from the rim. Dale glided out to meet it. Presently he saw a big sombrero, then a red, youthful face, above some evergreens. In another moment horse and rider came into view. Leveling his rifle, Dale called him to halt. The rider was unmistakably a young cowboy, and as cool as he could be. He complied with some range profanity. Then at second glance he drawled, "Howdy Brittenham."

"You've got the advantage of me, Mister Cowboy," retorted Dale curtly.

"Damn if I can see thet," he rejoined, with a smile that eased Dale's grimness.

"You know me," queried Dale.

"Shore, I recognized you. I've a pard, Jen Pierce, who's helped you chase wild horses. My name is Al Cook. We both ride for Stafford."

"You belong to Stafford's outfit?" asked Dale, lowering his rifle.

"Yep. We got heah before sunup this mornin'."

"How many of you an' where are they?"

"About twenty, I figger. Didn't count. Jud Larkin, our foreman, left five of us to watch thet far trail, up on top. He took the rest down."

"Where are they now?"

"I seen them just now. I can show them to you."

"Rustle. By gum, this is queer."

"You can gamble on it," returned Cook as he turned his horse. "We got tired waitin' for a showdown. I disobeyed orders an' rode around this side. Glad I did. For I run plumb across a trail fresh with tracks of a lot of horses. All shod! Brittenham, them hoss thieves have climbed out."

"Another trail? Hell! If thet's not tough . . . Where is it?"

"Heads in thet deep notch back of them cabins."

"They had a back hole to their burrow. Nalook didn't know thet."

"Heah we air," said the cowboy, sliding off. "Come out on the rim."

In another moment Dale was gazing down upon the grove of pines and the roofs of cabins. No men—no smoke! The camp site appeared deserted.

"Say, what the hell you make of thet?" ejaculated the cowboy, pointing. "Look! Up behind the thicket, makin' for the open grass! There's Larkin's outfit all strung out, crawlin' on their bellies like snakes!"

Dale saw, and in a flash he surmised that Stafford's men were crawling up on Strickland's. Each side would mistake the other for the horse theives. And on the instant a clear crack of a rifle rang out. But it was up on the rim. Other shots, from heavy short guns, boomed. That cowboy had run into the spying outlaws. Again the sharp ring of the rifle.

"Look!" cried the cowboy, pointing down.

Dale saw puffs of blue smoke rise from the green level below. Then gunshots pealed up.

"My Gawd! The locoed idiots are fightin' each other. But at thet, neither Nalook or Strickland would know Staffords outfit."

"Bad! Let me ride down an' put them wise."

"I'll go. Lend me your horse, you follow along the rim to the trail. Come down."

Dale ran back to leap into the cowboy's saddle. The stirrups fit him. With a slap of the bridle and a kick he urged the horse into a gallop. It did not take long to reach the trail. Wheeling into it, he ran the horse out to the rim, and then sent him down at a sliding plunge. He yelled to the cowboy on guard. "Brittenham! Brittenham! Don't shoot!" Then as the horse sent gravel and dust sky high, and, reaching a level, sped by the cowboy,

Dale added, "Look out for our men above!"

Dale ran the fast horse along the edge of the timber and then toward the thicket where he calculated Nalook would lead Strickland. He crashed through one fringe of sage and laurel, right upon the heels of men. Rifles cracked to left and right. Dale heard the whistle of bullets that came from Stafford's outfit.

"*Stop!*" he yelled, at the top of his lungs. "Horse thieves gone! You're fightin' our own men!"

Out upon the open grass level he rode, tearing loose his scarf. He held this aloft in one hand and in the other his rifle. A puff of white smoke rose from the deep grass ahead, then another from a clump of brush to the right, and next, one directly in front of him. The missile from the gun which belched that smoke hissed close to Dale's ear. He yelled with all his might and waved as no attacking enemy ever would have done. But the shots multiplied. The cowboys did not grasp the situation.

"No help for it!" muttered Dale with a dark premonition of calamity. But he had his good name to regain. He raced on right upon kneeling, lean-shaped cowboys.

"*Stop! Stop!* Horse thieves gone! You're fightin' friends! My outfit! Brittenham! Britt—"

Dale felt the impact of a bullet on his body somewhere. Then a terrible blinding shock.

When consciousness returned, Dale knew from a jolting sensation that he was being moved. He was being propped up in a saddle by a man riding on each side of his horse. His head sagged and when he opened his eyes to a blurred and darkened sight he saw the horn of his saddle and the mane of his horse. His skull felt as if it had been split by an ax.

His senses drifted close to oblivion again, then recovered a little more clearly. He heard voices and hoofbeats. Warm blood dripped down on his hands. That sensation started conscious thought. He had been shot, but surely not fatally, or he would not have been put astraddle a horse. His reaction to that was swift, and reviving with happiness. The faintness, the dizziness seemed to lessen, but the pain in his head grew correspondingly more piercing.

Dale became aware then that a number of horsemen rode with him. They began to crash through brush out into the open again where gray walls restricted the light. Then he felt strong hands lift him from the saddle and lay him on the grass. He opened his eyes. Anxious faces bent over him, one of which was Strickland's.

"My Gawd, men!" came to Dale in Rogers' deep voice. "It's Brittenham! Don't say he's—"

"Just knocked out temporarily," replied Strickland cheerfully. "Ugly scalp wound, but not dangerous. Another shot through the left shoulder. Fetch whiskey, bandages, hot water and iodine, if you have it."

"Aw!" let out Rogers, expelling a loud breath. He thumped away.

Dale lay with closed eyes, deeply grateful

for having escaped serious injury. They forced him to swallow whiskey, and then they began to work over him.

"You're the homesteader, Rogers?" Strickland queried.

"Yes. Me an' Britt have been friends. Knew each other over in the Sawtooth...Lord, I'm glad he ain't bad hurt. It'd just have killed thet Watrous girl."

"I'm Strickland," replied the other. "These fellows here are part of a posse I brought up from Halsey."

"Much of a fight? I heerd a lot of shootin'."

"It would have been one hell of a fight but for Brittenham. You see, the horse-thief gang had vamoosed last night. But we didn't know that. The Indian led us up on an outfit that had discovered us about the same time. We were crawling toward each other, through the thickets and high grass. The Indians began to shoot first. That betrayed our position and a lively exchange of shots began. It grew hot. Brittenham had gone up on the rim to scout. He discovered our blunder and rode back hell bent for election right into our midst. He stopped us, but the other outfit kept on shooting. Brittenham went on, and rode into the very face of hard shooting. He got hit twice. Nervy thing to do! But it saved lives. I had two men wounded besides him. Stafford's outfit suffered some casualties, but fortunately no one killed."

"What become of the hoss thieves?"

"Gone! After Reed and Mason had been killed, the gang evidently split. Some left in the night, leaving all their property except light packs. Sam Hood, one of Strickland's boys, killed two of them up on the rim, just before our fight started below."

"Ha! Thet ought to bust the gang for keeps," declared Rogers, rubbing his big hands.

"It was the best night's work this range ever saw. And the credit goes to Brittenham."

"Wal, I'll go fetch the wimmin," concluded Rogers heartily.

When, a little later, Dale had been washed and bandaged, and was half sitting up receiving the plaudits of the riders, he saw Edith come running out from under the trees into the open. She ran most of the way; then, nearing the cabin, she broke into a hurried walk and held a hand over her heart. Even at a distance Dale saw her big dark eyes, intent and staring. As she neared the spot where he lay surrounded by a half-circle of strange men, it was certain she saw no one but him. Reaching the spot where he lay, she knelt beside him.

"Dale!"

"Hellow—Edith," he replied huskily. "I guess I didn't bear such a charmed life after all. I sure got in the way of two bullets. But my luck held, Edith."

"Oh! You're not seriously injured?" she asked composedly, with a gentle hand on his. "But you are suffering."

"My head did hurt like h_ _ _ sixty. It's sort of whirlin' now."

"Rogers told me, Dale. That was a wonderful and splendid thing for you to do," Edith said softly. "What will Dad say? And won't I have Mister Stafford in a hole?"

Strickland interposed with a beaming smile. "You sure will, Miss Watrous. And I hope you make the most of it."

"Edith, I reckon we might leave for Bannock pronto," spoke up Dale eagerly. "I sent Nalook to tell your friends of your safety."

"Wal, Dale, mebbe I'll let you go tomorrow," chimed in Rogers.

"Don't go today," advised Strickland.

Next day Dale, despite his iron will and supreme eagerness to get home, suffered an ordeal that was almost too much for him. Toward the end of the ride two Bannock members of Strickland's posse were supporting Dale on his horse. But to his relief and Edith's poignant joy, he made it. At Bannock, medical attention and a good night's sleep made it possible for him to arrange to go on to Salmon by stage.

The cowboy Cook, who had taken a strong fancy to Dale, and had hung close to him, came out of the inn carrying a canvas-covered pack that Dale had him carefully stow under the seat.

"Britt, you sure have been keen about that pack. What's in it?" inquired Strickland with shrewd curiosity.

"Wouldn't you like to know, old-timer?"

"I've got a hunch. Wal, I'll look you up over at the Watrous Ranch in a couple of days. I want to go home first."

"Ahuh. You want to find out why those cowboy outfits didn't show up?"

"I confess to a little curiosity," replied the rancher dryly.

"Don't try to find out. Forget it," said Dale earnestly.

The stage, full of passengers, and driven by the jovial stage driver, Bill Edmunds, rolled away to the cheers of a Bannock crowd.

"Dale, what *is* in this pack under the seat?" asked Edith.

"Guess."

"It looked heavy, and considering how fussy you've been about it—I'd say—*gold*," she whispered.

Dale put his lips to her ear. "Edith, no wonder I'm fussy. I'm wild with excitement. That gang is broken up. An' I have Reed's money in my coat here—an' Mason's fortune in thet pack."

"Oh, how thrilling!" she whispered, and then on an after-thought she spoke out roguishly. "Well, in view of the—er—rather immediate surrender of your independence, I think I'd better take charge."

Darkness had settled down over the Salmon River Valley when the stage arrived at Salmon. Old Bill, the driver, said to Edith, "I reckon I'd better hustle you young folks out home before the town hears what Britt has done."

"Thad'd be good of you, Bill," replied Edith gratefully. "Dale is tired. And I'd be glad to get him home pronto."

They were the only passengers for the three miles out to the ranch. Dale did not speak, and Edith appeared content to hold his hand.

137

They both gazed out at the shining river and the dark groves, and over the moonlit range. When they arrived at the ranch, Dale had Bill turn down the lane to the little cabin where he lived.

"Carry this pack in, Bill, an' don't ask questions, you son-of-a-gun, or you'll not get the twenty-dollar gold piece I owe you."

"Wal, if this hyar pack is full of gold, you won't miss thet double eagle, you doggone lucky wild-hoss hunter."

"Thank you, Bill," said Edith. "I'll walk the rest of the way."

Dale was left alone with Edith, who stood in the shadow of the maples with the moon lighting her lovely face. He could hear the low roar of rapids on the river.

"It's wonderful, gettin' back, this way," he said haltingly. "You must run in an' tell your dad."

"Dad can wait a moment longer . . . Oh, Dale, I'm so proud—so happy—my heart is bursting."

"Mine feels queer, too. I hope this is not a dream, Edith."

"What—Dale?"

"Why, all thet's happened—an' you standin' there safe again—an' so beautiful. You just don't appear real."

"I should think you could ascertain whether I'm real flesh and blood or not."

Dale fired to that. "You'll always be the same, Edith. Can't you see how serious this is for me?" He took her in his arms. "Darlin', I reckon I know how you feel. But no words can tell you my feelins...Kiss me, Edith—then I'll try."

She was in his arms, to grow responsive and loving in her eager return of his kisses.

"Oh—Dale!" she whispered, with eyes closed. "I have found my man at last."

"Edith, I love you—an' tomorrow I'll have the courage to ask your dad if I can have you."

"Dale, I'm yours—Dad or no Dad. But he'll be as easy as that," she replied, stirring in his arms and snapping her fingers. "I hate to leave you. But we have tomorrow—and forever. Oh, Dale! I don't deserve all this happiness—kiss me good night...I'll fetch your breakfast myself. Kiss me once more...*Another!* Oh, I am—"

She broke from him to run up the lane and disappear under the moon-lit maples. Dale stood there a few moments alone in the silver-blanched gloom, trying to persuade himself that he was awake and in possession of his senses.

Next morning he got up early, to find the pain in his head much easier. But his shoulder was so stiff and sore that he could not use that arm. Having only one hand available, he was sore beset by the difficulty of washing, shaving and making himself as presentable as possible. He did not get through any too soon, for Edith appeared up the lane, accompanied by a servant, carrying a tray. She saw him and waved, then came tripping on. Dale felt his heart swell, and he moved about to hide his tremendous pride. He shoved a bench near the table under a canvas shelter that served for a porch. And when he could look up again, there she was, radiant in white.

"Mornin', Edith. Now I believe in fairies again."

"Oh, you look just fine. I'm having breakfast with you. Do you feel as well as you look?"

"Okay, except for my arm. It's stiff. I had a devil of a time puttin' my best foot forward. You'll have to do with a one-armed beau today."

"I'd rather have your one arm than all the two arms on the range," she replied gaily.

They had breakfast together, which to Dale seemed like enchantment. Then she took him for a stroll under the cottonwoods out along the river bank. And there, hanging on his good arm, she told him how her father had taken her story. Visitors from Salmon had come last night up to a late hour, and had begun to arrive already that morning. Stafford's outfit had returned driving a hundred recovered horses. Dale's feat was on the tip of every tongue.

"I didn't tell Dad about—about *us*, till this morning," she added finally.

"Lord help me! What'd he say?" gulped Dale.

"I don't know whether it was flattering or not—to me," Edith replied dubiously. "He said, 'That wild-horse tamer? Thank God, your hash is settled at last!'"

"He sure flatters me if he thinks I can tame

you. Wait till I tell him how you routed Bayne's outfit!"

"Oh, Dale, Dad was fine. He's going to ask you...But that'd be telling."

"Edith, if he accepts me, must I—will I have to wait very long for you?"

"*If!* Dad has accepted you, Dale. And honestly, he's happy over it...And as for the other—just what do you mean, Mr. Brittenham?"

"Aw! Will you marry me soon?"

"How soon?"

"I—I don't know, darlin'."

"Dale, dearest, I couldn't marry you with your head bandaged like that—or your arm in a sling," she said tantalizingly, as her dark eyes shed soft warm light upon him.

"But Edith!" he burst out. "I could take them off pronto. In less than a week!"

"Very well. Just that pronto." And with that they prepared to return to the Watrous ranch.

Watrous came out to meet them as they crossed the green. His face showed emotion and his eyes, at that moment, had something of the fire of Edith's. He wrung Dale's hand. But as befitted a Westerner, a little trace of his deep feeling pervaded his voice.

"Brittenham, I won't try to thank you," he said in simple heartiness.

"Thet suits me, Mr. Watrous. I'm kind of overwhelmed. An'—so I'd better get somethin'

out before I lose my nerve—I've loved Edith
since I came here first, three years ago. Will
you give her to me?"

"Dale, I will, and gladly, provided you live
here with me. I'm getting on, and since Mother
has been gone, Edith has been all to me."

"Dad, we will never leave you," replied
Edith softly.

"Bless you, my children! And Dale, there's a
little matter I'd like to settle right now. I'll
need a partner. Stafford has persuaded me to
go in big for the cattle game. I see its
possibilities. That, of course, means we'll have
cattle stealing as we have had horse stealing.
I'll need you pretty bad."

"Dad!" cried Edith in dismay. "You didn't
tell me you'd want Dale to go chasing cattle
thieves!"

"My dear, it might not come for years. Such
developments come slowly. By that time Dale
may have some grown cowboy sons to take his
place."

"Oh!" exclaimed Edith, plunged into sudden confusion.

"Dale, do you accept?" added Watrous,
extending his hand with an engaging smile.

"Yes, Mr. Watrous. An' I'll give Edith an'
you the best thet's in me."

"Settled! Oh, here comes Stafford. Lay into
him, youngster, for he sure has been nasty."

As Stafford came slowly down the broad
steps, Dale found himself unable to feel the
resentment that had rankled in him.

"Brittenham," said the rancher, as he
advanced, "I've made blunders in my life, but

never so stupid as the one regarding you. I am ashamed and sorry. It'll be hard for me to live this injustice down unless you forgive me. Can I ask that of you?"

"Nothin' to forgive," declared Dale earnestly, won by Stafford's straight forwardness and remorse. He offered his hand and gripped the rancher's. "Suspicion pointed at me. An' I took on Hildrith's guilt for reasons you know. Let's forget it an' be friends."

"You are indeed a man."

But when Stafford turned to Edith he had a different proposition to face. She eyed him with disdainful scorn, and stood tapping a nervous foot on the path.

"Edith, you can do no less than he. Say you forgive me, too."

"Yes, of course, since Dale is so kind. But I think you are a rotten judge of men."

"Indeed I am, my dear."

"And you're a hard man when you're crossed."

"Yes. But I'm a loyal friend. After all, this was a misunderstanding. You believed it, didn't you?"

"I never did—not for a minute. That's why I followed Dale."

"Well, you found him and brought him back." Stafford took a colored slip of paper from his pocket. He looked at it, then held it out to Edith. "I offered five thousand dollars reward for Brittenham, dead or alive. You brought him back alive—very much alive, as anyone with half an eye could see. And no wonder! It seems to me that this reward

143

should go to you. Indeed, I insist upon your taking it."

"Reward! But, Mr. Stafford—you—I," stammered Edith. "Five thousand dollars for *me?*"

"Surely. I imagine you will be able to spend it pronto. We all know your weakness for fine clothes and fine horses. Please accept it as a wedding present from a friend who loves you and who will never cease to regret that he mistook so splendid and noble a fellow as Dale Brittenham for a horse thief!"

STAMPEDE

The prairie was open, hot, dusty, and vast. Always the buffalo headed to the wind; they would drink and graze, and go on, noses to the breeze. If the wind changed overnight, in the morning they would be found turned round, traveling toward it. All day they grazed against it. They relied on their scent more than on sight or hearing; and in that open country the wind brought them warning of their foes. But for the great number of hide-hunters these buffalo might have escaped any extended slaughter.

The outfits were strung along the Brazos for many miles; and as the buffalo had to drink they were never far from water. Thus a number of hunters would get to them every day, kill many on the chase, and drive them on to the next aggregation of slayers.

Tom Doan had been in hard action for over two months. He and Pilchuck and Jones had killed thirty-nine hundred and twenty buffalo, losing only a small percentage of skins. Their aim was to last out the summer and fall, if their endurance could be great enough. They had no freighting to do now; they sold their hides in bales on the range.

The days grew to be nightmares. As the buffalo were driven up the river, then back down, and up again, the killing was accomplished for weeks in a comparatively small area. It got to be so that Tom could not ride many rods without encountering either a pile of bones, or a rotten carcass, or one just beginning to decompose, or a freshly skinned one torn over the night before by the packs of thousand of coyotes that followed the herd. Some days hundreds of newly skinned buffalo shone red along with the blackened carcasses over a stretch of miles. Buzzards were as thick as bees. And the stench was unbearable. The prairie became a gruesome, ghastly graveyard. The camps were almost untenable because of flies and bugs, ticks and mosquitoes. These hunters stuck to a job that in a worthy cause would have been heroic. As it was they descended to butchers, and each and all of them sank inevitably. Boom. Boom. Boom. All day long the detonation filled the hot air. No camp was out of hearing of the guns. Wagons lumbered along the dusty roads. All the outfits labored day and night to increase their store of hides, riding, chasing, shooting, skining, hauling, and pegging, as if their very lives depended upon incessant labor. It was a time of carnage.

Long had Tom Doan felt the encroachment of a mood he had at one time striven against— a morbid estimate of self, a consciousness that this carnage would debase him utterly if he did not soon abandon it. Once there had been a wonderful reason for him to give up the hunting. Milly Fayre. Sometimes her dark eyes still haunted him. If she had not been lost, he would long ago have quit this bloody game. The wound in his heart did not heal. Love of Milly abided, and that alone saved him from the utter debasement of hard life at a hard time.

One morning when he drove out on the dust-hazed, stinking prairie, he found a little, red, buffalo calf standing beside its mother that Tom had shot and skinned the day before. This was no new sight to Tom. Nevertheless, in the present case there seemed a difference. These calves left motherless by the slaughter had always wandered over the prairie, lost, bewildered; this one, however, had recognized its mother and would not leave her.

"Go along. Get back to the herd," yelled Tom, shocked despite his callousness.

The calf scarcely noticed him. It smelled of its hide-stripped mother, and manifestly was hungry. Presently it left off trying to awaken this strange, horribly red and inert body, and stood with hanging head, dejected, resigned, a poor miserable little beast. Tom could not drive it away; and after loading the hide on the wagon, he returned twice to try to make it run off. Finally he was compelled to kill it.

This incident boded ill for Tom. It fixed his mind on this thing he was doing and left him no peace. Thousands and thousands of beautiful little buffalo calves were rendered motherless by the hide-hunters. That was to Tom the unforgivable brutality Calves just born, just able to suck, and from that to yearlings, were left to starve, to die of thirst, to wander until they dropped or were torn to

147

shreds by wolves. No wonder this little calf showed in its sad resignation the doom of the species.

August came. The great herd massed. The mating season had come, and both bulls and cows, slaves to the marvelous instinct that had evolved them, grew slower, less wary, heedless now to the scent of man on the wind.

At the beginning of this mating time it was necessary to be within a mile or less to hear the strange *roo roo roo-ooo*. This sound was the bellow of a bull. Gradually day by day the sound increased in volume and range. It could be heard several miles, and gradually farther as more and more bulls bellowed in unison. *ROO ROO ROO-OOO*—It became incessant, heard above the boom—boom— boom of guns.

The time came when it increased tremendously and lasted day and night. Tom Doan's camp was then ten miles from the herd. At that distance the bellow was as loud as distant thunder. *ROO ROO ROO-OOO*. It kept Tom awake. It filled his ears. If he did fall asleep, it gave him nightmares. When he awoke he heard again the long mournful roar. At length it wore upon him so deeply that in the darkness and solitude of night he conceived the idea he was listening to the voice of a great species, bellowing out for life.

This wild, deep *Roo-ooo* was the knell of the buffalo. What a strange sound, vastly different from anything human, yet somehow poignant, tragic, terrible. Nature had called to the great herd; and that last million of buffalo bellowed out their acceptance of the decree. But in Tom's morbid mind he attributed vastly more to this strange thunder, which was not the trampling thunder of their hoofs. In the dead of night, when the guns were silent he could not shake the spell. It came to him then how terribly wrong, obsessed, evil were these hide-hunters. God and nature had placed the wonderful beasts on earth for a purpose, the least of which might have been to furnish meat and robe for men in a measure of reason. But here all the meat was left to rot, and half the hides. The remaining half went to satisfy a false demand, and to make rich a number of hunters, vastly degraded by the process.

Roo-ooo-ooo. Tom heard in that the meaning of a futile demand of nature.

Tom Doan and Pilchuck reined their horses on the crest of a league-sloping ridge and surveyed the buffalo range.

To their surprise the endless black line of buffalo was not in sight. They had moved north during the night. At this early morning hour the hunters were just riding out to begin their day's work. No guns were booming, and it appeared that Tom and the scout had that part of the range to themselves.

"Wal, we spent yesterday peggin' hides in camp, an' didn't think to ask Jones if the buffalo had moved," remarked Pilchuck, reflectively.

"The wind has changed. It's now from the north," said Tom.

"Shore is. An' the buffs will be grazin' back

pronto. That is, if they are grazin'."

"Any reason to doubt it?" asked Tom.

"Wal, the breedin' season's just about ended. An' that with this muggy, stormy, electric-charged mornin' might cause a move. Never in my huntin' days have I seen such a restless queer herd of buffalo as this one."

"No wonder" exclaimed Tom.

"Wal, it ain't, an' that's a fact...Do I see hosses yonder?"

Tom swept the prairie with his glass.

"Yes. Hunters riding out. I see more beyond. They're all going down river."

"Come to think of it, I didn't hear much shootin' yesterday. Did you?"

"Not a great deal. And that was early morning and far away," replied Tom.

"Buffs an' hunters have worked north. Let's see. The river makes a bend about ten miles from here, an' runs east. I'd be willin' to bet the herd hasn't turned that bend."

"Why?"

"Because they'll never go north again. For two months the trend has been south, day by day. Some days a wind like yesterday would switch them, but on the whole they're workin' south. This ain't natural for midsummer. They ought to be headed north. 'Course the mob of hunters are drivin' them south."

"But how about today?" inquired Tom.

"Wal, I'm shore figgerin'. Reckon I can't explain, but I feel all them outfits ridin' north will have their work for nothin'."

"What will we do?"

"I'm not carin' a lot. Reckon I've sickened on this job, an' I shore know that, when I stay a day in camp."

Tom had before noted this tendency in the scout. It was common to all those hunters who had been long in the field. He did not voice his own sentiment.

"I've been wantin' to ride west an' see what the next ford is going to be like," said the scout, presently. "We'll be breakin' camp an' movin' south soon. An' the other side of the river is where we want to be."

For the first time Tom experienced a reluctance to a continuation of the old mode of traveling south. Why not turn north once more? The thought was a surprise. There was no reason to start north, unless in answer to the revulsion of hide-hunting. This surely would be his last buffalo hunt. But he did not think it just to his partners to quit while they wanted to keep on. His reflection then was that Pilchuck was wearing out, both in strength and in greed.

They rode west, aiming to reach the river some four or five miles farther on.

It was a cloudy, sultry summer morning, with storm in the air. The prairie was not a beautiful prospect. Tom seemed to gaze over it rather than at it. Westward the undulating gray rise of ground stretched interminably to a horizon bare of landmarks. Far in the east rays of sunlight streamed down between sullen, angry, copper and purple-hued clouds.

The north threatened. It was black all along the horizon. Still, oppressive, sultry, the air seemed charged.

From time to time Pilchuck turned in his saddle to gaze backward along the empty range, and then up at the cloud bank. It appeared to Tom as if the scout were looking and listening for something..

"What're you expecting?" queried Tom, yielding to curiosity. "A thunderstorm?"

"Wal, I'll be darned if I know," ejaculated Pilchuck. "Shore I wasn't thinkin' about a storm. Wasn't thinkin' at all. Must be just habit with me ... But now you tax me, I reckon I'm uneasy about that herd."

Pilchuck led west farther than he had calculated, and struck the river at a wonderful place where the prairie took a sudden dip for miles, sheering steeply to the shallow water. Here was the buffalo ford, used by the herds in their annual migrations. Trees were absent, and brush and grass had not the luxuriance common to most stretches of river bank. From prairie rim to margin of river sloped a long steep bank, even and smooth; and at one point the wide approach to the ford was split and dominated by a rocky eminence, the only high point in sight along the river.

The place seemed dismal and lonely to Tom, as he sat on his horse while Pilchuck forded the river. Contrary to most river scenes, this one was lifeless. Not a bird or animal or a fish or turtle in sight. Loneliness and solitude had their abode in this trodden road of the buffalo.

At length the scout returned and rode up to Tom.

"Wal, I wouldn't care to get a team stuck in that sand," he remarked. "It shore ain't packed none...Lend me your glass."

The scout swept a half-circle of the horizon, and finally came to a halt westward, at a point on the prairie some distance from the river.

"See some small bunches of buffalo," he said. "Let's ride up on them, make our kill, skin what we get, an' pick them up with the wagon on our way south tomorrow."

"You're the boss," replied Tom.

"Wal, I wish some one was bossin' me," returned Pilchuck, enigmatically.

They trotted off over the gray prairie, and after traveling a couple of miles could see the buffalo plainly. Meanwhile a slight breeze began to blow from the north.

"I'll be darned," ejaculated Pilchuck with annoyance, "Wind's turned again. If it blows stronger we'll not slip up on this bunch."

Another mile brought increase of wind, and the wary buffalo, catching the scent of the killers, loped away over the prairie. Pilchuck watched them in disgust. "Run, you old dunder-heads. Run clear across the Rio Grande...Tom, I reckon we're all spoiled by the past easy huntin'. It'll never be easy again. An' somehow I'm glad. Let's work back."

They turned about to face the breeze, now quite strong,. cooler, with a heavy scent of rotting buffalo carcasses.

"Faugh!" exclaimed the scout. "I'd rather have nose an' eyes full of cottonwood smoke."

Tom's quick ear caught a very low rumble of thunder. He turned his head. The sound had ceased. It had come on a stronger puff of wind.

"What'd you hear?" inquired the scout, whose eye never missed anything.

"Thunder."

"Wal, it does look stormy. But I never trust thunder in this country," replied the scout, significantly.

He halted his horse, and Tom did likewise. They gazed at the north. Dull, leaden, mushrooming clouds were moving toward them, not rapidly, but steadily, in heavy changing forms. They merged into a purple-black mass down which streaked thin zigzag ropes of lightning.

"Storm all right," observed Pilchuck. "Listen."

After a moment in which nothing was heard save the heaving of horses, the rattle of bridle, and a creak of leather, the scout dismounted.

"Get off, Tom, an' walk away from the horses ... Listen now."

Presently Tom again heard the low dull rumble.

"There," he said.

"Shore. That's genuine thunder, an' it means rain for this stinkin' dusty hot range ... Listen some more, Tom."

The two men stood apart, Pilchuck favoring his right ear, Tom his left. They remained motionless. Several times the mutter of thunder, distinct now to Tom, caused the scout to nod his head.

"Reckon that's not what I'm expectin'," he said, gloomily. "An' we've no time to stand here all day...Listen hard, Tom. You're younger than me."

Tom's sluggish blood quickened a little. He had been two years with this old plainsman, during which there had been numberless instances of his sagacity and vision, and remarkable evidences of experience. Pilchuck was worrying about that herd of buffalo. Thereupon Tom bent lower, held his breath, and strained his ear with all intensity possibly. Again he heard the muttering long rumble—then the beat of his heart, the stir of his hair over his temple—the sweep of wind. Thunder again. That was all; and he abandoned the strain.

"Nothing but storm," he told Pilchuck.

"I reckon my ears are old, an' my imagination makes me think I hear things," returned the scout. "But a moment ago...Try again. I want to be shore."

Thus incited, Tom lent himself to as sensitive and profound listening as was possible for him. This time he seemed to hear the thunder as before, somewhat louder; and under it another fainter sound, an infinitely low roar that did not die out, that went on and on, deadened by another mutter of thunder, and then, when this was gone, beginning again, low, strange, unceasing.

Then he straightened up and told Pilchuck what he had heard. How sharply and intelligently the scout's gray eyes flashed! He made no reply, except to raise one of his brawny hands. Leaving it extended, he froze in the attitude of an Indian listening. Tom again lent his ear to the strengthening breeze. Thunder—then a long, low menacing roar—thunder again—and roar. He made his own deductions and, lifting his head, waited for the scout to speak. Long did Pilchuck maintain that tense posture. He was a slow, deliberate man on occasions. Sometimes he would act with the most incredible speed. Here he must have been studying the volume, direction, distance of this thrilling sound, and not its cause. Suddenly his big brown hand clenched and shot down to crack into the palm of the other. He wheeled to Tom, with gray lightning in his eyes.

"Stampede! The whole herd," he ejaculated. "I've been expectin' it for days."

Then he gazed across the northern horizon of the prairie round to a point due east.

"You notice we can see only four or five miles," he said. "The prairie rises slow for about that distance, then dips. That'd deaden sound as well as hide any movin' thing. We can't be shore that herd is far away... Funny how we run into things. Reckon we'd better ride."

They mounted, and were off at a gallop that gave place to a run. Tom had lost his fleet, faithful Dusty, and was now riding a horse strong and sound and fairly fast, but no match for Pilchuck's hunter. So Tom fell behind gradually. He did not goad the horse, though he appreciated Pilchuck's brief hint of danger.

The scout rode east, quartering toward the river, and passed a couple of miles out from where he and Tom had stopped at the ford. Tom gradually fell behind until he was fully a quarter of a mile behind. As long as he could keep Pilchuck in sight he did not have any anxiety about the separation. The horse could run, and he was sure-footed. Tom believed he would acquit himself well even in a grueling race with the buffalo. It seemed strange to be running away from an unseen danger. While riding he could not hear anything save the rhythmic beat of hoofs and rush of wind. He observed that the direction Pilchuck had chosen was just a point east of the center of the black storm cloud. Far to its right showed the dim fringe of river timber. There was a wide distance between the end of that cloud and the river, most of which was gently sloping prairie. He had a keen eagerness to know what could be seen beyond the long ridge-top.

Next time he gazed at Pilchuck he was amazed to see him pulling his horse to a halt. Tom rode on with eyes now intent. The scout reined in and leaped out of the saddle. He ran a few paces from the horse, and stopped to lie flat on the ground. Tom realized that Pilchuck was listening with ear close to the earth. The action startled Tom. Not improbably, this situation was growing serious. Pilchuck lay a moment, then got up and stood like a statue. Then he abruptly broke his rigid posture and leaped astride. But instead of riding off he waited there, face to the north. Tom rapidly overhauled him and pulled his mount to a stand.

"Jude, what's wrong?" he called, sharply.

"I ain't shore, but I'm damned scared," replied the scout.

"Why? I can't see or hear anything."

"See that yellow dust way to the right of the black sky. Look. It's movin'—I'm afraid if we go farther this way, we'll get headed off an' run into the river. We could cross, but it'd take time, an' when we got over we might have to run south. That'd never do. We've got to go east or west."

"Jude, I hear a roar," said Tom.

"Shore. So do I. But it was the movin' dust that stopped me...Keep still now an' let me figger. If I've any prairie cunnin' left we're in a hell of a fix. We've got to do what's right—an' quick."

Therefore Tom attended to sight of the low, rounded, yellow cloud of dust. It did move, apparently slowly, and spread to the right. Against the background of purple sky it held something ominous. Tom watched it rise gradually to the left, though in this direction it did not spread along the prairie so rapidly. The ground sloped that way, and the ridge-top stretched higher then the level to the east, where the dust now rolled plainly. The roar was a dull distant rumble, steady and ear-filling, though not at all loud. It was a deceiving sound, and might be closer than it seemed or farther away.

"Doan, look," he shouted, in a tone Tom had

never heard. His voice seemed to merge into a rolling rumble.

Tom wheeled. Along the whole of the prairie horizon had appeared a black, bobbing line of buffalo. Above them rose the yellow dust, and beyond that spread the stormcloud of purple. The ragged front of the herd appeared to creep over the ridge-top, like a horizon tide wide, low, flat, black. Toward the west the gray level horizon was being blotted out with exceeding swiftness, as the herd came in sight. It spread like a black smoke, flying low. To the east the whole space noted by Tom before had been clouded with black and yellow. The front line of the herd, then, did not appear to be straight across. It was curving from the right.

One moment Tom gazed, rapt, thrilling, then his blood gushed hot. The great herd was at last on the stampede. Not five miles distant, running downhill.

"By God, we're in a trap," yelled Pilchuck, hoarsely. "We've only one chance. Follow me an' ride."

He spurred and wheeled his horse and, goading him into a run, headed for the river ford. Tom spurred after him, finding now that his horse, frightened by the roar, could keep up with Pilchuck's. They ran straight away from the eastern front of the herd, that was curving in and quartering away from the western front. Tom had ridden fast before, but Pilchuck's start bade fair to lead him into the swiftest race of his experience on the range. He was aware of drawing away somewhat from the roar in the rear; on his right, however, the sound augmented. Tom gazed around. His eyes, blurred from the rush of wind, showed a league-wide band of black, sliding down the prairie slope, widening, spreading. He did not look behind.

Pilchuck's fleet horse began to draw ahead. The old scout was riding as he had never ridden away from Comanches. Tom remembered what fear these old plainsmen had of the buffalo stampede. It was the terror of the plains, more appalling than the prairie fire. Comanches could be fought; fires could be outridden or back-fired, but the stampede of buffalo was a rolling sea of swift, insane beasts. With spur and fist and voice Tom urged his horse to its utmost, and kept the distance between him and Pilchuck from widening further.

Both horses were now on a headlong run, strained to the breaking point. The wind hissed by Tom's ears, swayed him back in his saddle. On both sides the gray prairie slid by, indistinct, a blurred expanse, over which he seemed to sail. He could not see the river depression, but before long he made out the rocky eminence that marked the site of the ford. Pilchuck's intention was now plain. At first Tom had imagined the scout meant to try to cross the river ahead of the herd; now, however, he was making for the high point of rock. This realization unclamped Tom's cold doubt. If the horses did not fall they could make that place of safety. Pilchuck was fifty feet ahead, and not only was he driving the horse at breakneck speed, but he was guiding him over what appeared to be the smoother ground. Tom caught the slight variations in the course and the swervings aside; and he had only to follow.

So they flew. The gray mound of rock seemed close, the prairie flashing by, yet how slowly the distance lessened. Tom saw Pilchuck turn. His brown face gleamed. He waved his hand. A beckoning and an encouragement. Peril was not over, but safety was in sight. Then the scout leaned back, pulling the horse to his haunches, on which he slid to a stop. Over Pilchuck's head Tom saw the pale brightness of water. The river. Behind Tom rolled a rumbling thunder, strange to hear with his ears full of rushing wind. He dared not look back.

The straining horse broke his stride, caught it again, stretched on, and plunged to the bare rise of rocky ground. Tom hauled with all his strength on the bridle. He checked the maddened animal, but could not stop him. Pilchuck stood ten feet above the bank. He had dismounted. Both hands were uplifted in gesture of awe. Tom leaped off just as his horse slowed before the first rocky bench. Dragging him up, Tom climbed to Pilchuck, who seemed to yell at him. But Tom heard no voice. The rocky eminence was about half an acre in extent, and high enough above the bank to split the herd. Tom dropped the bridle and whirled in fear and wonder.

His first thoughts when he saw the ragged, sweeping tide of beasts, still a third of a mile distant, was that he would have had time to spare. The herd had not been so close as his imagination had pictured.

Pilchuck dragged Tom, pulling him higher on the rock. The scout put his mouth close to Tom's ear and manifestly yelled. But Tom heard no voice; felt only a soundless, hot breath. His ears were distending with a terrific thunder. His eyes were protruding at an awful spectacle.

Yet he saw that sweep of buffalo with a marvelous distinctness, with the swift leap of emotion which magnified all his senses, Across the level front of his vision spread a ragged, shaggy black wall of heads, humps, hoofs, coming at the speed of buffalo on the stampede. On a hard run. The sea of bobbing backs beyond disappeared in a yellow pall of dust curled aloft and hung low, and kept almost the speed of the front rank. Above the moving mantle of dust, farther back, showed the gray pall of storm. Lightning flashed in vivid white streaks. But there was no thunder from above. The thunder rolled low, along the ground.

Spellbound, Tom gazed. He was riveted to the rock. If he had not been he would have fled, up, back, away from that oncoming mass. But he could only gaze, in a profound consciousness of something great and terrifying. These buffalo might not split round the higher ground; those in line might run over the rock. What an end for hide-hunters. Killed, crushed, trampled to jelly, trampled to dust under the hoofs of the great herd. It would be just retribution. Tom felt the awful truth of that in his lifting heart. It was mete. The murderous hide-hunters, money-grubbers, deserved no pity. He could not feel any for himself. How furiously angry that curling surf of woolly heads and shiny horns and gleaming hoofs. On. On. On. The thundering herd. How magnificent and appalling.

Suddenly his ears ceased to function. He could no longer hear. The sense had been outdone. There was no sound. But he saw yet the mighty onsweep, majestic, irresistible, an army of maddened beasts on the stampede, shaking the earth. The rock under his feet began to tremble. It was no longer stable. He felt the queer vibrations, and the sensation added to his terror.

Transfixed, Tom awaited the insupportable moment for the rolling front ranks to reach the rock, either to roll over it like a tidal wave, or split round it. The moment was an age. Pilchuck was holding to him. Tom was holding to Pilchuck. The solid earth seemed about to cave in under them. Shaggy black heads bobbing swiftly, gleam of horns, and flash of wild eyes, hoofs, hoofs, hoofs sweeping out, out, out—and the awful moment was at hand.

The shaggy flood split round the rock and two streams of rounded woolly backs, close-pressed as water, swift as a mill-race, poured over the bank toward the river.

Pilchuck dragged Tom away from the back position to the front of the rock. As if by supernatural magic the scene was changed.

Below, far on each side, the mass of buffalo spilled over the embankment to plunge into the river. Up and down the water line spread white splashes; and over and into them leaped the second ranks of buffalo, too close to miss the first. Then, what had momentarily been ranks on the slope, closed up into a solid mass of black. Bulge and heave—great sheets of muddy water—a terrible writhing massing forward along that irregular front. Then the tide of buffalo swept on, over, once more a flat, level multitude of heads and humps, irrepressible as an avalanche. They crossed the river on the run; the stampede had been only momentarily retarded. Downriver, below the ford, far as eye could see, stretched lines of buffalo swimming, swiftly, like an endless flock of enormous geese. Upriver stretched the same, as far as eye could see. The slope of the prairie to the water was one solid mass of buffalo, moving as one beast, impelled by motive as wild as the action. Above swept the dust, blowing as a storm wind from the prairie, and, curling like a yellow curtain of smoke, it followed the buffalo across the river, up the long slope, and out upon the prairie.

Tom and Pilchuck were on that level between the moving dust above and the moving buffalo below. All view back toward the prairie whence the herd rolled was soon obliterated. Likewise the front ranks of the great mass disappeared on the opposite side, under this accompanying mantle. But the river, for awhile, lay clear to their gaze, miles up and miles down, and all visible space of water and ground was covered with buffalo. Buffalo more numerous than a band of ants on the march.

Tom sank down, overcome by the spectacle, by the continuous trembling of the earth under him, by the strangulation which threatened, by the terrible pressure on his eardrums.

Suddenly night seemed to intervene. A gale swooped the dust away across the river; and in place of a yellow curling curtain of dust there came a slanting gray pall of rain. It blackened as the light grew less. Blazing streaks of lightning played through the gray gloom. But if there was thunder above it, it could not be heard in the thunder below.

Pilchuck drew Tom under a narrow shelf of rock, where, half-protected from the deluge, they crouched in the semi-darkness. What seemed hours passed. Yet there was no end to the passing of the great herd. The rain ceased, the sky lightened and cleared, and clearer grew the black mantling of prairie and river. All was buffalo, except the sky. Then the sun broke out of the clouds.

Tom's stunned senses rallied enough for him to appreciate the grandeur and beauty suddenly given the scene by a glorious sheen of gold and purple, streaming down from the rifts between the clouds. The dust was gone. The thousands of shining black backs moved on and on, rapidly, ponderously, swallowed up by haze of the disappearing storm. And still the buffalo came over the prairie, obscuring the ground.

But at last the time came when the mass showed breaks in the ranks, and then, in the rear line, more ragged than had been the fore. Tom's hearing seemed gradually to be restored. That, he realized, was only the diminishing of the vast volume of sound to the point where it was no longer deafening. It was a blood-deadening thunder that gradually lessened as the end of the herd rolled on from the prairie, down over the bank, and across the river.

The thundering herd swept on out of sight. And the thunder became a roar, the roar a rumble, and the rumble died away.

Pilchuck rose to his lofty height and peered across the river, into the gray haze and purple distance that had swallowed up the buffalo. He seemed to be a man who had lived through something terrible.

"The last herd," he said, with pathos. "They've crossed the Brazos an' they'll never come back... The storm of rain was like the storm of lead that'll follow them."

Tom also got dizzily to his feet and faced the south. What he felt about the last herd could not be spoken. He had been spared a death he felt he deserved; and he had seen a mighty spectacle, incalculable in its spiritual effect. All in vain was the grand stampede of that thundering herd. It must drink, it must graze—and behind would troop the ruthless hunters of hides. But Tom had seen and felt its overpowering vitality, its tremendous life, its spirit. Never would he kill another buffalo. And a great sadness pervaded his mind. As he stood there, trying to form in words something to say to Pilchuck, a huge old buffalo bull, one of the many that had been mired in the sand, floundered and wallowed free, and waddled to the opposite shore. Stupidly he gazed about him, forlorn, alone, lost, a symbol of the herd that had gone on without him. Then he headed south out into the melancholy gray of the prairie.

"Jude, I'm—going—north." exclaimed Tom, haltingly, full of words that would not come.

"Shake," replied the old scout, quick as a flash, as he extended his brawny hand.

THE REVENGE OF TODDY NOKIN
By Zane Grey

THE REVENGE OF TODDY NOKIN

Toddy Nokin was a Piute Indian Chief, proud and independent. Though he had little use for most of the wranglers who came to Wild Horse Mesa to steal the Indian's horses and despoil their women, he saw in the maverick, Chane Weymer, a different breed of man. Chane's greatest ambition was to capture Panquitch, the legendary wild stallion who had fired the imagination of horse wranglers all over the west. Chane had saved Toddy's teenage daughter, Soci from the attentions of a dissolute wrangler named Manrube. Toddy had vowed to help Chane capture the great stallion, while Manrube had sworn revenge. In the climax of this swiftly moving story, Chane subdues Panquitch only to lose him to Manrube, who has trapped Chane and his beautiful fiancee, Sue Melberne, along with the great stallion in a rugged Utah canyon. How they are rescued in the dark and bloody climax, makes this one of the most thrilling Zane Grey stories.

Chane rode Brutus down the dark-walled portal into the rocky maze of the canyon country.

This he meant to be the first of an exhaustive exploration of every possible place that could be an exit or egress of the wild horses to and from Wild Horse Mesa; yet, as it was by no means uncertain that he might not meet Panquitch at any time, he was prepared for such a momentous event. He carried two lassoes on his saddle. Presently he dismounted, and taking several burlap sacks he had brought with him, he cut them up, and folded them thick, and tied them securely round the big hoofs of Brutus. Chane did not want to make noise going down the canyon, or leave any tracks. Brutus looked on rather impatiently while this was being done, as if he could like to know what was wrong with his hoofs. Then Chane mounted again and rode on.

It was still early in the day, for now and then the white sun shone above in the narrow gap between the lofty rims. Chane felt that he would have leisure today and the following days to explore every nook and cranny under the mysterious wall of the great mesa. Brutus walked noiselessly over the rocks and left no trace. Chane avoided the sand bars. If the wild horses were out on top and should come down to see horse tracks in the sand of their secret passageway to and from the mesa, they might, under the leadership of Panquitch, at once turn back. Chane remembered wonderful instances of the intelligence, almost reasoning power of wild stallions. The longer a stallion was hunted the keener and wilder he became. Panquitch had outwitted a hundred wild-horse wranglers. But that had been in open country. Here, deep in these narrow canyons, with their abrupt turns and deep waterways, he would be decidedly at a disadvantage. Chane had not in the least been tempted to bring Alonzo to help him, though he acknowledged the superiority of the *vaquero*. Chane had the wild-horse hunter's strange ambition, so far as a great stallion was concerned: he would corner and rope Panquitch unaided.

As Chane progressed down the canyon he paid strict attention to only those places where a crack in the wall, a branch canyon, or a wide enlargement might hide a possible means of exit to the rim above. It was astonishing what careful investigation brought to light. Chane found places where he might have climbed out on foot, but where Brutus, agile as he was, could not follow.

At length he reached the big park-like oval, the expansion of the canyon where in his memorable flight across the rivers and out of this labryinth he had encountered Panquitch with his band. Near the upper end of this huge oval Chane dismounted to walk along the stones at the edge of the sandy bars, and worked back to where the water disappeared. He found horse tracks, made, he was sure, the day before. They came to the water and went back toward the low rise of red slope. This point was not where he had encountered

Panquitch. That, Chane remembered, was a beautiful constriction of this enlargement of the canyon, a bowl-like place, full of cotton-woods and willows.

Chane studied the whole opposite wall, as far as he could see. He could see perhaps a mile of this oval. Just opposite where he stood a wide break in the wall came down to the sand. It was smooth and worn rock, widening like a fan toward the wavy summit of yellow ridges. These he knew were the round knolls so marked when one gazed down upon the canyon country from the rims. Beyond and above, of course, rose Wild Horse Mesa, but Chane could not get a glimpse of it. He noted how the wavy red rock spread beyond and behind bulges of the wall, that to the left and right of him sheered down perpendicularly to his level.

That one to the right of him held his studious attention because he believed it hid much from his gaze. This huge frowning section of canyon wall lay between the slope opposite him and the one below where he had watched Panquitch climb. It looked to Chane as if the wild horses could come down one slope and go up the other. Then he remembered the narrow gleaming walls and the long deep pools of water. Surely the wild horses could not swim these except when on the way out to the upland country above, or when they were returning to their mysterious abode. Chane decided that it would take days to get a clear map in his mind of this maze.

Returning to Brutus, he rode on down the

171

oval, keeping to the curve of wall, far from the center. As he rode he got higher, and farther back, so that his view of the slope opposite was better. Soon, however, the bulge of intervening wall shut out his view entirely of that slope. Then he attended more keenly to what lay ahead.

The oval park ended in a constriction like the neck of a bottle. The sunlight came down from a marvelous slope of red rock. This slope he recalled so well that he felt a thrill. Here was where he had watched Panquitch climb out. A dark cleft, *V*-shaped, split the ponderous bulk of the cliff at the end of the oval. It was still far off, but Chane recognized it. Down in there was where he hoped some day to meet Panquitch. His hope was merely a dream, he knew, for the chances were a thousand to one that he would ever have such luck.

"Reckon I'll leave Brutus and climb that slope," soliloquized Chane.

Whereupon he rode on down past the break in the wall toward the grove of cottonwoods. Here there was shade and patches of green grass. As Chane dismounted Brutus lifted his head and shot up his ears, in the action that was characteristic of him when he heard something unusual.

"Hey! What'd you hear, old boy?" queried Chane, suddenly tense.

A distant hollow sound seemed to be filling Chane's ears. But it might have been just the strangeness of the canyon wind, like the roar of the sea in a cave. Chane waited, slowly losing his tensity. But he observed that Brutus lost nothing of attentiveness. Chane trusted the horse, and desiring to get under cover he drew Brutus in among the cottonwoods, and selected a place where he could see in all directions without being seen, and have at least one hidden exit, down into the V-shaped cleft. Chane remembered Manrube and Bud McPherson, enemies of his from long back.

Brutus turned so that he could head up the canyon, and only Chane's hand and low voice kept him still. The keener ears or nose of the horse had reacted to something Chane could not yet detect.

All at once a weird, horrid blast pealed out, not far from Chane, and higher than where he stood. The echoes bellowed from wall to wall. Chane, seeing that Brutus was about to neigh, clasped his muzzle with strong pressure.

"Keep still," whispered Chane, fiercely.

He had never heard a sound so uncanny and fearful. It made his blood creep, and for a second he sustained a shock. Then his quick mind solved the realization that in this country nothing but a horse could peal out such a cry. Therefore, when it was followed by light quick clatter of hoofs, Chane was not at all surprised.

"Brutus, we've heard that before," he whispered, patting the horse.

Chane was several hundred yards from where the slope merged into the level canyon floor, and the lower part of it, owing to the cottonwoods, was hidden from his sight. But wild horses were surely coming down, and they might turn to enter the *V*-shaped cleft instead of up the canyon. Something had frightened them.

"By golly!" he muttered. "This's a queer deal." He wanted much to linger there and see the wild horses, but instead of staying he leaped on Brutus and, riding close to the wall, under protection of the cottonwoods, he made quick time to the end of the grove. Here lay sections of wall that had broken from above. At the mouth of the cleft Chane rode Brutus behind a huge boulder, and dismounting there; he peeped out.

This point of vantage, owing to the curve of the wall taking him out and away from the restricted view in the cottonwoods, gave him command of the canyon.

He was just in time to get a glimpse of red and black and bay mustangs entering the cottonwoods from the slope.

Far up that wavy incline he espied a slight figure, moving down. He could scarcely credit his eyes. Did it belong to an Indian? Yet the quick lithe step stirred his pulse! He had seen it before, somewhere. Dark hair streamed in the breeze.

"*Sue!*" whispered Chane, in utter astonishment. "Well, I'll be—she and Chess have wandered up there. They're having fun chasing wild horses. But where's he?"

Chane could not see that part of the slope to his right, for a projection of overhanging wall hid it from sight.

Then a band of wild horses burst from the cottonwoods, out into the open sandy space of several acres. They were trotting, bunched close, frightened but not yet in panic. Presently, far out on the sand bar they halted, heads up, uncertain which way to go.

From the far side of them Panquitch appeared, trotting with long strides, something in his leonine beauty and wildness, his tawny black-maned beauty, striking Chane as half-horse and half-lion.

Certain it was that sight of him that sent a gush of hot blood racing over Chane. His mind seemed to be trying to overcome the tense and vibrating sensation, to grasp at some strange fatality in the moment. Here he hid. Panquitch was there, not a quarter of a mile away. If Chess, his old pard, should happen to be on the other side of that band of wild horses they could run pell-mell down toward the V-shaped cleft. Chane's hand shook as he pressed it close on the nose of the quivering Brutus.

Panquitch trotted in front of his band, to one side and then the other, looking in every direction. He did not whistle. To Chane he had the appearance of a stallion uncertain of his ground. He looked up the slope, at the girl coming down, choosing the easiest travel from her position, now walking, now running, and working toward a bulge of cliff. Then Panquitch gave no further heed to Sue. He was sure of danger in that direction. He trotted out to the edge of the sand bar and faced down, his head high, eager, strained, wild.

"By golly! I'm afraid he's got a whiff of me and Brutus!" whispered Chane. "What a nose he has! The wind favors us. Now, I want to know why he doesn't make a break up the canyon."

Panquitch wheeled from his survey down the canyon to one in the opposite direction. His action now showed that his suspicions were strong in this quarter. His great strides, his nervous halting, his erect tail and mane, his bobbing head, proved to Chane that he wanted to lead his band up the canyon, but feared something yet unseen.

A sweet, wild, gay cry pealed down from the slope.

Chane espied Sue standing on the bulging cliff, high above the canyon floor, and she was flinging her arms and crying out in the exultance of the moment. Chane saw the sunlight on her face. He strained his ears to distinguish what she was voicing to the wildness of the place and the beautiful horses that called it home.

"Fly! Oh Panquitch fly!" she was singing to the wind, in the joy of her adventure, in the love of freedom she shared with Panquitch.

Chane understood her. This was girlish fun she was having, yet her sweet, wild, cry held the dominant note of her deeper meaning. She loved Panquitch, and all wild horses, and yearned for them to be free.

"Girl, little do you dream you may drive Panquitch straight into my rope," muttered Chane, grimly.

The stallion suddenly froze in his tracks, making a magnificent statue typifying fear. A whistling blast escaped him. The nature of the hollow walls must have given it tremendous volume. It pealed from cliff to cliff, and then, augmented by united whistles from the other horses, it swelled into a deafening concatenation.

Chane's keen eye detected Chess up the canyon, bounding into view. At the same instant Panquitch wheeled as if on a pivot and leaped into headlong stride down the canyon, with his band falling in behind him.

Like a flash Chane vaulted into the saddle. He sent Brutus flying over stones and through water into the cool shadow of the cleft. Any narrow place to hide, from behind which he could rope the stallion! All Chane's force went into the idea. A jutting corner tempted him, as did another huge rock, but the gleam of water drew him on. One of the deep long pools lay just ahead. Brutus padded on at tremendous gait. The canyon narrowed, darkened, and more than once Chane's stirrup rasped on the wall.

Full speed, Brutus charged into the pool and plunged through shallow water. To his knees, to his flanks, he floundered on—then he went into deep water, going under all but his head. How icy the water to Chane's heated blood! He gazed back. Not yet could he see any movement of wild horses.

Fifty yards ahead the straight wall heaved into a corner, round which the stream turned in a curve. If Chane could find footing for Brutus behind that corner, Panquitch would have no chance. What a trap! Chane reveled in the moment. The wildest dream of his boyhood was being enacted.

He did not spare Brutus, but urged him, spurred him, beat him into tremendous action. The swelling wave made by the horse splashed on the walls. Brutus reached the corner—turned it. Chane reined him into the wall. There was a narrow bench, just level with the water. But that would be of no help unless Brutus could touch bottom. He did. Chane stifled a yell of exultation. Fate was indeed against Panquitch. Brutus waded his full length before he reached the ledge. He was still in five feet of water, and on slippery rocks. Chane had no time to waste. The cracking of hoofs up the canyon rang like shots in his ears. Panquitch and his band were coming. Chane needed room to swing his lasso. Should he get out on the ledge or stay astride Brutus? Both plans had features to recommend them. But it would be best to stay on Brutus.

Chane turned the horse round. Brutus accomplished this without slipping off the rocks into deep water.

"Brutus, what do I want with Panquitch when I have you?" Chane heard himself whisper. He did not need Panquitch. It was his hunting instinct and long habit.

Then Chane had burst upon him the last singular fact in the string of fatalities which now bade fair to doom Panquitch. The important thing at the climax here was to have room to cast the lasso. Chane had felt the nearness of the corner of wall. He had planned to urge Brutus into the water the instant Panquitch appeared. But this need not be risked. There was no necessity to get beyond the corner of wall.

Chane was left-handed. He threw a noose with his left hand, and in the position now assumed he was as free to swing his rope as if he had been out in the open.

The trap and the trick were ready. Chane's agitation settled to a keen, tight, grim exultation. Nothing could save Panquitch if he ever entered that deep pool. Chane listened so intensely he heard his heartbeats. Yes! He heard them coming. Their hard hoofs rang with bell-like clearness upon the boulders— then the hollow muffled sound of hoofs on rock under the water—then the splashing swish!

Soon the narrow canyon resounded to a melodious din. Suddenly it ceased. Chane realized the wild horses had reached the pool. His heart ceased to beat. Would the keen Panquitch, victor over a hundred clever tricks to capture him, shy at this treacherous pool? Clip—clop! He had stepped out into the water. Chane heard his wild snort. He feared something, but was not certain. The enemies behind were realities. Clip—Clop! He stepped again.Clip—Clop! Into deeper water he had ventured—then a crashing plunge!

It was followed by a renewed din of pounding hollow hoof-cracks, snorts, and splashes. They were all taking to the pool.

Chane swung the noose of his lasso round his head, tilting it to evade the corner of wall.

It began to whiz. His eyes were rivited piercingly upon the water where it swirled gently in sight from behind the gray stone. Brutus was quivering under him. The plunging crashes ceased. All the wild horses were swimming. The din fell to sharp snuffing breaths and gentle swash of water. A wave preceded the swimming band.

A lean, beautiful head slid from behind the wall, with long black main floating from it. Panquitch held his head high.

At that short distance Chane could have roped one of his ears. Even in the tremendous strain Chane could wait a second longer. Panquitch was his.

The stallion saw Brutus and his rider—the swinging rope. Into the dark wild eyes came a terror that distended them. A sound like a horrid scream escaped him. He plunged to turn. His head came out.

Then Chane cast the lasso. It hissed and spread, and the loop, like a snake, cracked over Panquitch, under his chin and behind his ears. One powerful sweep of Chane's arm tightened that noose.

"Whoopee!" yelled Chane, with all the power of his lungs. "He's roped! He's roped! Panquitch! Oh!—ho! ho! He's ours, Brutus, old boy. After him, old boy!"

Panquitch plunged back, pounding the water, and as Chane held hard on the lasso the stallion went under. Chane clacked the rope, and urged Brutus off the rocks. Pandemonium had begun round that corner of wall. As Brutus soused in and lunged to the middle of the stream, Chane saw a sight he could never forget.

Upwards of a score of wild horses were frantically beating and crashing the water to escape back in the direction they had come. Some were trying to climb the shelving wall, only to slip, and souse under. They bobbed up more frantic than before, screaming their terror. Some were trying to climb over the backs of those to the fore. All were in violent commotion, and uttering some variation of horse sounds.

Panquitch, hampered by the lasso, was falling behind. Chane pulled him under water, then let him come up. Brutus had to be guided, for he tried to swim straight to the stallion. Chane did not want that kind of a fight. It was his purpose to hold Panquitch in the pool until he was exhausted. With that noose round his neck he must tire sooner than Brutus. This unequal struggle could not last long. Chane had no power to contain his madness of delight, the emotion roused by the feel of Panquitch on the other end of the lasso. Panquitch, the despair of Nevada wranglers long before he had shown his clear heels to those of Utah! Panquitch roped! It was incredible good fortune. It was the great moment of Chane's wild life.

"Aha there, old lion-mane," he called, true even in that moment to his old habit of talking to horses. "You made one run too many! You run into a rope! Swim now! Heave hard! Dive, you rascal! You're a fish. Ho! Ho! Ho!"

But when Panquitch plunged round to

make for his adversaries the tables were turned. Chane's yell of exultation changed to one of alarm, both to frighten Panquitch, if possible, and to hold Brutus back. Both, however, seemed impossible. Brutus would not turn his back to that stallion. His battle cry pealed out. Chane hauled on the lasso, but he could not again pull Panquitch under.

Despite all Chane could do, the stallion and Brutus met in head-on collision. A terrific battle ensued. Chane was thrown off Brutus as from a catapult. But he was swift to take advantage of this accident. A few powerful strokes brought him round to Panquitch, and by dint of supreme effort astride the back of the wild stallion.

Chane fastened his grip on the ears of the stallion, to lurch forward with all his weight and strength. He got the head of Panquitch under the water.

"Back! Back!" yelled Chane to Brutus.

It was a terrible moment. Chane preferred to let Panquitch free rather than drown him. But if Brutus kept fighting on, crowding the stallion, Chane saw no other issue. Under him Panquitch was shaking in convulsions. Chane let go of his head. The stallion bobbed up, choking, snorthing. But if terror was still with him it was one of fury to kill. He bent his head back to bite at Chane. His eyes were black fire; his open mouth red and dripping; his teeth bared. Chane all but failed to keep out of his reach.

In his cowboy days Chane had been noted for his ability to ride broncos, mean mustangs, bucking horses, mules, and even wild steers. The old temper to ride and conquer awoke in him. Fighting the stallion, beating Brutus off, keeping his seat, Chane performed perhaps the greatest riding feat of his career. He had, however, almost to drown the stallion.

At length Panquitch, suddenly showing signs of chocking, headed for the shallow water. His swimming was laborious. Chane loosed the tight rope, then plunging off he swam back to Brutus and got in the saddle. He urged Brutus faster and faster, to pass the sinking Panquitch. Not a moment too soon did Brutus touch bottom, and plunging shoreward, he dragged Panquitch after him. The stallion could no longer breathe, yet he staggered out of the shallow water, to the sand, where he fell.

Chane leaped off Brutus to fall on Panquitch and loosen the lasso. The stallion gave a heave. He had been nearly choked to death; perhaps the noose had kept water out of his lungs. His breast labored with a great intake of air. Then he began to shake with short quick pants.

"Aw, but I'm glad!" ejaculated Chane, who for a moment had feared a calamity. But Panquitch would revive. Chane ran back to the heaving Brutus, and procuring a second lasso from the saddle, he rushed again to the stallion and slipped a noose round his forelegs.

"Reckon that's about all," he said, rising to survey his captive.

Panquitch was the noblest specimen of horseflesh Chane had ever seen in all his wandering over the rangelands of the west. But in these flaming black eyes there was a spirit incompatible with the rule of man. Panquitch might be broken, but his heart would ever be wild.

He could never love his master. Chane felt pity for the fallen monarch, and a remorse. He was killing something, the like of which dwelt in his own heart.

"Panquitch, it wasn't a square deal," declared Chane. "I played you a dirty trick. I'm not proud of it. And so help me God I've a mind to let you go."

So the wild-horse hunting instinct in Chane found itself in conflict with an emotion compelled into existence by the defeat and prostration of the great stallion. Chane missed that crowning joy of the wild-horse wrangler—to exhibit to the gaze of rival hunters a captive horse that had been their passion to catch and break and ride.

"Wo—hoo! Oh, Chane, I'm coming!" called a girlish high-pitched voice, pealing along the narrow walls.

Sue appeared at the mouth of the cleft, standing upon a boulder, with her hair shining in the sun. She had espied him and Brutus from afar, and perhaps had guessed the issue. Then Chess's voice rang down the canyon.

"What you-all doing, Chane Weymer?"

He caught up with Sue, and lending her a

hand, came striding with her over the rock benches. He had lost his hat.

Chane heard them talking excitedly, out of breath, wondering, tense and expectant. Brutus whistled. Then Chess and Sue came out of the shadow, into the strip of sunlit canyon. They saw Panquitch lying full length on the sand. Chess broke from Sue and came rushing up. One glance showed him Panquitch was alive.

"Good Lord!" he screeched, beside himself with excitement, running to grasp Chane and embrace him. He was sweating, panting, flushed of face, wild of eye. "Panquitch! And you got him hawg-tied!"

He ran back to the stallion, gazed down upon him, moved round him, gloated over him. "Hurry, Sue! Come! Look! Will you—ever believe it? We chased—Panquitch right—into Chane's trap! Of all the luck! Hurry to see him! Oh, there never was such a horse!"

Then he strode back to Chane, waving his hands. "We climbed that slope—back there," he went on. "Just for fun. Wanted to see. Then from up on top—I spied the wild horses. Sue saw Panquitch first. We ran down—having fun—seeing how close we could get. Then Sue said: 'Run down ahead, Chess. I'll stay here. Turn them—chase them by me—so I'll get to see Panquitch close.' So I ran like mad. Queer place up there. I headed them. They ran back—up over that hollow—behind the big knob of wall. Right over that by Sue! I saw her run down the slope—this way. But I made for

185

the canyon. Just wanted to see them run by. Couldn't see them. I ran some more. Then the whole bunch trotted out of the cottonwoods. Panquitch lorded it around. He was prancing. He didn't know which way to run. I heard Sue screaming at him. Then Panquitch bolted this way—and his bunch followed...just think! You were here. You saw them. You must have hid.... You roped Panquitch! Chane, you owe it all to Sue. She drove Panquitch to you."

"I reckon," replied Chane, conscious of unfamiliar riot in his breast. "Where'd the bunch go—when they ran back?"

"Passed me—like the wind," panted Chess. "Straight up the canyon."

"You don't say!" exclaimed Chane, in surprise. "I thought they'd take to one of the slopes. Chess, these wild horses have more than one outlet to their burrow."

Sue had held back, and was standing some ways off, staring from the prostrate Panquitch to Chane. Her hands were pressed over a heaving bosom. Her eyes seemed wide and dark. There was something about her that made Chane catch his breath. This was not Sue Melberne as he knew her.

"Come on, Sue," called Chess. "Nothing to fear. Panquitch has ropes on him."

"Oh, it's all my fault—my fault," cried Sue, pantingly, as again she hurried toward them, keeping away from the fallen stallion. "Is he hurt? He breathes so—so hard."

"Reckon Panquitch's only choked a little,"

186

replied Chane. "You see, I roped him in the water. Brutus and I had to follow. Panquitch got mad and charged up. I couldn't manage Brutus. He wanted to fight. So they had it hot and heavy. I was knocked off Brutus. But I swam to Panquitch, straddled him, and had to hold his head under water to keep him from drowning us both."

"You're all bloody! You're hurt," replied Sue, coming to him.

Chane had not noted the blood on his hands and his face. Evidently he had been scratched or barked in the struggle.

"Guess I'm not hurt," he said, with a laugh, as he drew out his wet scarf. "Here, Chess, hold the rope while I tie my cuts. If Panquitch tries to get up just keep the rope tight."

Chess received the lasso and drew it taut. "Hyar, you king of stallions," he called out. "You've sure got tied up in the wrong family. We're bad *hombres*, me and Chane. Just you lay still."

Chane became aware that Sue had come quite close to him.

"Let me do it," she said, taking the scarf. And without looking up she began to bind his injured hand. She was earnest about it, but not at all deft. Her fingers trembled. Chane, gazing down upon her, saw more signs of agitation. Under the gold-brown of her skin showed a pearly pallor; the veins were swelling on her round neck. Her nearness, and the unmistakable evidences of her distress and exctiement, shifted the current of Chane's mind. How momentous this day! What was the vague portent that beat for entrance to his consciousness?

Sue finished binding his hand, and then she looked up into his face, not, it seemed, without effort. She was strained with the exertion and excitement of this adventure. But would that have accounted for a subtle difference in her?

"There's a cut on your temple," she said, and untying her own scarf she began to fold it in a narrow band. Her blouse was unbuttoned at the neck, now exposing the line where the gold tan met the white of her swelling bosom. "Bend your head," she added.

Chane did as he was bidden, conscious of mounting sensations. The soft gentle touch of her hands suddenly inflamed him with a desire to seize them, to kiss them, to press them against his aching heart. Stern repression did not, however, on this occasion, bring victory. He had no time to think. It was like being leaped upon in the dark—this attack of incomprehensible emotion.

"There—if you put your sombrero on carefully—it will stay," she said.

"Thanks. You're very good. Reckon I'm not used to being doctored by tender hands," he replied, somewhat awkwardly, as he drew back from her. That was what made him unsure of himself—her nearness. Strange to him, then, and growing more undeniable, was the fact that as he retreated she followed, keeping close to him. When she took hold of the lapel of his vest and seemed fighting either for command of herself or strength to look up again, then he realized something was about to happen.

"I'm all wet," he protested, trying to be natural. But he failed. It was not a natural moment or situation or position for them.

"So you are I—I hadn't noticed it," she said, and instead of drawing away she came so close that her garments touched him. Even this slight contact caused Chane to tremble. "Chane, come a little away—so Chess won't hear," she concluded, in a whisper.

Chane felt as helpless in her slight hand as Panquitch now was in his. She led him back a few paces, in the lee of a slab of rock that leaned down from the wall.

"What's—all this?" he demanded, incredulously, as she pushed his back against the rock.

"It's something very important," she replied, and then she fastened her other hand in the other lapel of the vest. She leaned against him. The fact was so tremendous that Chane could scarcely force his faculties to adequate comprehension of it. Yet there came to his aid an instinct natural to him through all the strenuous and perilous situations of his desert life, and it was a kind of cool anger of self-preservation.

"Yes?" he queried, doubtfully.

She was quite pale now and the pupils of her dark eyes were dilating over deep wonderful shadows and lights. He felt her quiver. His response was instantaneous and irresistible, but it was a response of his heart, not his will. He would never let her know what havoc this contact played with him.

"Would you do something great for me?" she whispered, her husky voice betraying a dry mouth.

"Great!" he ejaculated. What little control he had when one word could throw him off his balance! "Why, Sue Melberne, I reckon, I would—for you—or any girl, if I could."

"Not for any other girl," she returned swiftly. "For *me!*"

"I'll make no rash promises. What do you want?"

"Let Panquitch go free."

Chane could only stare at her. So that was it! Sudden relief flooded over him. What might she not have asked? How powerless he was to refuse her most trivial wish! But she did not know that. This longing of hers to see Panquitch freed was natural and he respected her, liked her, loved her the more for it. Easy now to understand her white face, her soulful eyes, her quivering lips and clinging hands! She loved wild horses. So did he, and he could see her point of view. Alas for the strange vague rapture that her close presence had roused! But he could prolong this delicious moment of torment.

"Are you crazy, girl?" he demanded.

"Not quite," she replied, with a wistful smile that made him wince. "I want you to let Panquitch go. It was my fault. I was his undoing. I longed to see him close—to scream at him—to watch him run. So I drove him into your trap."

"Quite true. I'd never have caught him save for you. But what's that? I don't care. Once in my life I had a wrangler's luck."

"Something tells me it'll be bad luck, unless you give in."

Chane felt as if about to fall from a height. What was this all about? His wounded heart probed! Yet did it matter?

Chane had a glimpse of her eyes filming over, glazed, humid, before she closed them. Her head, that had been tilted back, drooped a little toward him, and her slender body now lent its weight against his. Chane had no strength to tear himself away from her, nor could he bear this close contact longer. The poor girl was overwrought, all because of sentiment about a horse.

"Sue, what ails you?" he demanded, sharply, and he shook her.

His voice, his rudeness, apparently jarred her out of her weakness. It seemed he watched a transformation pass over her, a change that most of all nonplused him. A blush rose and burned out of her face, leaving a radiant glow. She let go of his vest, drew back. And suddenly she seemed a woman, formidable, incredible, strong as she had been weak, eloquent of eye.

"Something did ail me, Chane, but I'm quite recovered now," she replied, with a wonderful light on her face.

"You talk in riddles, Sue Melberne."

"If you weren't so stupid you'd not think so."

"Reckon I am stupid. But we've got off the trail. You asked me to let Panquitch go."

"Yes, I beg of you."

"You're awful set on seeing him walk off up that slope, aren't you?" he inquired, trying to find words to prolong the conversation. He despised himself for longing to have her come close again, to appeal to him. Presently he must tell her that her slightest wish could never be ignored, that Panquitch was hers to free.

"Chane, I'll do anything for you if only you'll let him go."

He laughed, almost with bitter note. "How careless you are with words! No wonder Manrube got a wrong hunch."

She flushed at that, and lost for a second the smile, the poise that so baffled him. But swiftly they returned.

"I was a silly girl with Manrube," she replied. "I'm an honest woman now...I said I'll do anything for you, Chane Weymer— *anything*."

"Reckon I hear you, unless I'm locoed," he said, thickly. "I'm not asking anything of you. But I'm powerful curious. If you're honest now, suppose you tell me a few of the things you'd do for me."

"Shall I begin with a lot of small things—or with something big?" she inquired, in so sweet and tantalizing a voice that Chane felt the blood go back to his heart. She was beyond

192

him. How useless to match wits with any woman, let alone one whom a man adored madly and hopelessly. Chane felt he must get out of this. One more moment, then she could have Panquitch!

"Well, suppose you save time by beginning with something big," he suggested, in a scorn for himself and for her. It was a farce, this talk, all except her earnest appeal and her sweetness. He could not argue with her, nor follow her subtleties.

She stepped close to him again. And then Chane shook with a sense of impending catastrophe. She seemed cool, brave, and honest as she claimed to be. But her dark eyes held a strange fire.

"Very well. The biggest thing a woman can do is to be a man's wife."

Stupefaction held Chane in thrall. It took a moment to recover from the shock of that blow. He had heard her speak. He was not out on the lonely desert, listening to the voices of the cedars. All about Sue Melberne belied that slow, sweet, cool speech. Suddenly a fury of bewilderment, of uncertainty, assailed Chane. Laying powerful hands on her shoulders he shook her as he might have a child.

"You'd marry me to save that horse?" he demanded, incredulously.

"Yes."

"You'd throw yourself away for Panquitch?" he went on, sternly.

"Yes. But—I'd hardly call it that."

"Sue Melberne, you'd be my—my *wife!*" The very idea of such fortune made Chane mad.

He released her. He wrestled with himself. Thick and heavy his heart beat. It mattered not why or how he might possess this girl, but the fact that he might was maddening. Still he fought for the right. What a sentimental, unexplicable girl!

"Yes, I will, Chane," she said.

"You love Panquitch so well. I remember you risked much to free the wild horses in the trap corral. But this is beyond belief. Yet you say so . . . You don't look daft, though your talk seems so. I can't understand you. To sacrifice yourself for a horse, even though it's Panquitch!"

"I wouldn't regard it as—sacrifice," she whispered.

"But it is. It'd be wrong. It'd be a crime against your womanhood. I couldn't accept it. Besides, you're doing wrong to tempt me. I'm only a poor lonely rider. I've always been hungry for a woman. And I've never had one . . . It's doubly wrong, I tell you."

Chane stamped up and down the narrow place behind the rock. Hard violent action in the open had been his life; he brought it to bear on the conflict in his breast. With a black, hot, tearing wrench he got rid of the spell.

"Sue, I brought this—on myself," he said, gentle of tone, though his voice broke. "I wanted to hear you beg for Panquitch. I wanted you to be close to me. It was madness. All the time I was lying. For the moment you asked me to free Panquitch I meant to do it. You helped me catch him. You can free him."

Sue walked straight to him, closer than

before, almost into his arms. The poise of head, the radiance of face, the eloquence of eye—these had vanished and she seemed stranger than before, a pale thing reaching for him.

"That will make me happy, but only if I can pay my debt," she faltered.

"What *do* you mean?" demanded Chane, harshly.

"If you free Panquitch you must make me—your wife."

"Are you out of your head or lying to me?"

"Both," she whispered, and fell against him.

Chane clasped her in his arms, and held her closer and closer, sure in his bewilderment of only one thing, that if she persisted she would break him down. But now she was in his arms. Her head drooped so that he could not see her face, but she was stirring, turning to him, sinking on his breast. Never could he let her go now! It was all so astounding. His mind and body now seemed to leap to the sweetness of possession. The golden amber sunlight of the canyon moved about him like a glory of lightning, and it was certain that thunder filled his ears. He was realizing what he could not believe. The stunning truth was that Sue Melberne lay in his arms, strangely willing. That was enough for his hungry heart, but his conscience stormed at him. Then, last of all, he felt as in a dream Sue's arms go up around his neck and fasten there.

"My God!" he gasped. "Sue, this can't be for Panquitch."

Her face came up, white like a flower, wet with tears. But strain and strife were gone.

"If you had any sense you'd have known I—I loved you!"

"Sue Melberne!"

"Now, my wild-horse hunter, take your rope off Panquitch—and put it on me," she replied, and raised her lips to his.

A little later Chane took the rope out of Chess's hands and held it to Sue. Then he knelt to slip off the noose of the other lasso, the one that was tied to the saddle on Brutus. Swiftly Chane stripped this from the stallion.

"Hey! What you doing?" yelled Chess, in amazement. "He's come to. The son-of-a-gun will be on his feet in a jiffy."

Chane apparently took no note of Chess's concern. This moment was full of unutterable joy in that he was making Sue happy and slipping his rope off Panquitch—freeing the last wild hose he would ever capture. Bending over the stallion he loosed the knot round the forelegs.

"Pull it—easy," he called to Sue.

Chess actually leaped up in the air, to come down with cracking boots.

"What—the hell!" he cried, piercingly.

Sue drew the lasso taut, and slid it gently from the stallion. He gave a fierce snort. Then he raised his head. Actually he looked at his legs, and then with muscles knotting all over his body he heaved hard and got up. He was free and he knew it. Hate and fear flamed in his bloodshot eyes. Chane thrilled when he met that look and knew in his soul what he was giving up. Panquitch stood for a moment, with his breathing audible. Thus Chane saw him close, standing unfettered, in all his magnificent and matchless beauty. Indeed, he was a lion of wild horses. Perfect in build, perfect in color, the rarest combination and the only one Chane had ever seen in a tawny shade of yellow, with flowing mane and tail black as night. He had not a scar, not a blemish, not a fault. He represented the supreme handiwork of nature—a creature too beautiful, too proud, too noble, too wild for the yoke of man.

Panquitch shook himself and moved away. He was still weak, but his spirit showed in his prance. He snorted fiercely at Brutus. And Brutus returned the challenge.

"Run—Oh, Panquitch, run!" cried Sue, with rich and mellow sweetness in her voice.

But the stallion did not run. His slow action was that of a spent horse. Keeping to the middle of the canyon, he trotted on, by the sand patch where lately he had pranced so proudly, by the cottonwood grove and the wavy slope of rock, and on, out of sight.

Then Chess exploded. He cursed, raved, he glared, not for a full moment becoming intelligible.

"You let him go! Panquitch, the greatest wild horse in the world. You had him. You could have given him to me. I've no great horse like Brutus. I always wanted one...Let him go for Manrube to rope! Or some damned lucky rider who'll happen on him before he recovers... Oh, you're locoed. The two of you.

Sue, you're a sentimental fool. Chane, you're a damn fool ... I could cry. Chane, whatever has come over you?"

"Chess, I reckon I'm no longer boss of the Weymer outfit," replied Chane, striving to keep undue pride and joy out of his words, but failing utterly.

"Hey?" ejaculated Chess, as if he had been struck. His mouth opened wide, likewise his eyes, and he made a picture of stupidity and incredulity.

"Little Boy Blue, I'm sure going to be your sister," said Sue, with all of gladness.

Suddenly transfigured with rapture, Chess made at them.

Chane strode up the canyon as one in a dream, leading Brutus, with Sue in the saddle. From time to time he looked back to see if she were a reality. Her dark eyes shone, her lips were parted. There was a smile on her face, an exquisite light, a spirit that must be the love she had confessed. Life had become immeasurably full and sweet for him.

Chess had passed from every manner of congratulation, boastfulness as to his bringing about this match, delight in Chane's good fortune, back to his former despair at the loss of Panquitch.

"Now you two have each other, you don't care for nothing," he growled, with finality, and forged on ahead to leave them alone.

It appeared to be about the middle of the afternoon when the amber light of the canyon began to tinge with purple. The breeze had ceased and the air was warm. Less tremendous grew the looming walls, wider the stream of blue sky overhead, lower the rims, and therefore the oppressiveness began to wane, and the sense of overpowering weight and silence.

In many places showed the fresh tracks of the wild horses, last of which were those of Panquitch. He was following his band, on the way to the uplands. Chane would have preferred that they had turned off at the wavy slope below and were now safe under the lee of Wild Horse Mesa. Panquitch, in his spent condition, would hardly be able to escape a fast rider. Still, Chane's exalted mind could not harbor misgivings or doubt, or anxiety, not on this day in which he had been lifted to the kingdom of happiness.

Chess strode on with his head bent, his gaze on the tracks of Panquitch, and he passed out of sight round a bend in the canyon.

Many times Chane halted to let Brutus come abreast of him, so that he could look up at Sue or touch her. And all at once something which had been forming in his mind coalesced into an insupportable query.

"Sue, when will you marry me?"

She laughed happily. "Why, we've only just become engaged," she replied roguishly.

"Darling, this is the wild canyon country of Utah," he protested. "People only stay engaged in cities or settlements."

"We'll really be pioneers, won't we?"

"Yes. But I shall always see that you go into

civilization every summer, for a visit...Tell me, how long must I wait?"

A rosy glow vied with the gold of Sue's warm cheek. "Surely until Uncle Jim comes," she said, shyly.

"Your uncle! I remember now—he's a preacher. And he may come yet this fall, certain in the spring?"

"I wish I could fib to you," returned Sue, "and say spring. But dad is sure Uncle Jim will come by Thanksgiving."

He pressed her hand, unable to utter his profound joy and gratitude. Then he took up the bridle and strode on, leading Brutus. He saw the widening canyon, the sand bars cut up by many hoofs, the lowering rims, the shallow brook, yet he was not conscious of them, for he walked as one in a trance.

The time came when ahead the canyon made a curve into brighter light. Beyond this point was the junction of the four canyons where camp had been made. As Chane turned the corner Brutus shied so violently that he tore the bridle from Chane's grasp.

"Hands up, Weymer," called a rough, husky voice.

Chane's dream was rudely shattered. More than once he had heard the ominous note which rang now in his ears. He was unarmed. He raised his hands, and at the same instant he saw a dark-bearded man, with leveled gun, stide from behind the cliff.

"Up they are," he said, and ground his teeth in sudden impotent anger. Then he recognized the man. "Howdy, Slack."

"Same to you, Weymer," replied the other, sliding round in front of Chane toward Brutus.

"Reckon you see I'm not packing a gun."

"Yep, I shore was glad you wasn't wearin' any hardware. But just keep your hands up an' a respectable distance. I'm a distrustful fellar," replied Slack, and presently, getting within reach of Brutus, he secured the bridle.

Chane's line of vision, as he stood rigidly, did not include Sue, until Slack led Brutus forward. Then she appeared, white of face and mute in her fear. Manifestly she had no thought of herself, but of the gun Slack held leveled at Chane.

"Mosey on in front, Weymer," ordered the outlaw.

Chane had no choice but to comply. He had been in situations before, and this one would not have greatly perturbed him if Sue had not been there. He lowered his hands and strode on towards the camp, intensely curious to see if what he found there would be identical with what he expected.

The triangular space of intersecting canyons presently came unobstructed to his view. A campfire was burning, and several men surrounded it, one of them sitting. Even at considerable distance Chane recognized the hard lean face of Bud McPherson.

Chess sat on a stone to one side, with his hands tied behind his back. But Sue's father, Melberne, did not appear to be present.

"Oh, there's Panquitch!" burst out Sue, in shrill distress.

Chane, shocked at Sue's exclamation, saw a number of horses, all saddled, standing bridles down, to the left of the campfire group.

"Look! Look!" cried Sue, as if choking.

As Chane did not know where she was looking and did not care to take too many risks with Slack, he shifted his gaze in search of the stallion.

"Chane! Look!" screamed Sue, this time with fury and horror.

"Manrube! Manrube! He's got a rope on Panquitch!"

The content of her words flashed on Chane just as he espied Manrube hanging on two lassoes that were fast on Panquitch. The great stallion was holding back with a spirit vastly in excess of his strength.

Many as had been the bitter moments of Chane's life that was the bitterest. Sue's cry of anguish rang in his ears. The wild horse which she had loved and freed was now in the power of a hated rider. It was a blow that to Chane struck home acutely. Panquitch, spent from his fight in the canyon pool, and expending what little strength he had left to catch up with his band, had fallen easily into Manrube's clutches. The cheap and arrogant rider probably had not even credited his capture to the weakened condition of the stallion. He was crowing like a game cock over his prize, with his braggart's and bully's air more pronounced than ever. He whipped the ropes that secured Panquitch, making the horse flinch. The effect of this on Chane was to distort his vision with passion and hate, so that it seemed for a moment he was gazing through a blood-red haze.

"Oh-h!" cried Sue, now deep and poignantly. "He's hurting Panquitch. I won't stand it."

"Sue, keep still," ordered Chane, sharply. "We can do nothing."

"Hyar, you squallin' bobcat," growled Slack, "stop walkin' your hoss on my heels."

They reached the campfire, with Chane a little in the lead. One of the other men, whose face was familiar but whose name Chane could not recall, drew a gun and pointed it at him.

"Bill, he ain't got no gun, but your idea is correct," drawled Slack, and turning to Sue he laid a rough and meaning hand upon her, which she repulsed in anger. Then Slack swore at her and pulled her out of the saddle.

"Say, wench, if you know when you're well off, you'll be sweet instead of catty," he declared.

On the moment, when the other men were haw-hawing at Slack's sally, Chane happened to catch Sue's eye and conveyed to her in one glance the peril of the situation.

"Howdy, Weymer," said Bud McPherson, cooly. "I'm savin' some of your good grub."

"Howdy, Bud. It's a habit of yours to help yourself to other people's property," rejoined Chane. This outlaw was the most dangerous of the group, Chane decided, though he knew little of the two strangers who had followed Manrube from Wund. But McPherson, though a horse thief and a bad man, had elements that Manrube and the others did not show. He was not little.

Back of the campfire, near where Chess sat bowed and disconsolate, crouched another man, also tied, and he appeared a pretty worn and miserable object. Chane at last recognized the unshaven and haggard face.

"Loughbridge!" he ejaculated, in both amazement and satisfaction. "Well, what're you hawg-tied for? Reckoned you'd thrown in with this outfit."

"Weymer, I was fooled worsen Melberne," said Loughbridge. "I took Manrube at his brag. I had no idea he was a hoss thief—"

"Stop your gab!" yelled Manrube, stridently. "You're a white-livered liar. I'm not a horse thief."

"Bud, give it to me straight," said Chane. "What's the deal with Loughbridge?"

"Wal, it ain't so clear to me," replied McPherson, wiping his mouth and scant beard and rising to his feet. "Somebody gimme a smoke...Fact is, Weymer, I wasn't keen on havin' this man thrown in with us. Wal, when he found out our plan to appropriate Melberne's stock—which shore come out at this camp—he hedged an' began to bluster. You know I never argue. So we just put a halter on him."

"Where's Melberne?" added Chane.

"Shore you ought to know. We're waitin' fer him."

"Then what?" demanded Chane.

"Weymer, you allus was a hell-bent-pronto

hombre," declared McPherson, with good humor. "Reckon you want to know bad what the deal is. Wal, I'll tell you. We've been loafin' in camp waitin' for you-all to ketch the last bunch of hosses before fall set in cold. Then we seen them two Piutes prowlin' around, an' we figgered they'd fetched you another bunch of mustangs. Wal, the deal is hyar. When Melberne comes we'll rustle back to his homestead an' relieve you all of considerable hoss wranglin' an' feedin' this winter."

"Then, next summer, you'll look us up again," asserted Chane, with sarcasm.

"Haw! Haw! You shore hit it plumb center," rejoined the ruffian.

"Bud, you're no fool," said Chane, seriously. "You can't keep up this sort of thing. Somebody will kill you. Why don't you cut loose from these two-bit wranglers you've been riding with? I've known horse thieves to go back to honest ranching. It paid."

McPherson had no guffaw or bandinage for this speech of Chane's. It went home. His frankness relieved Chane. McPherson would hardly resort to blood-spilling unless thwarted or cornered. Chane felt greatest anxiety on behalf of Sue. The outlaw leader, however, had never struck Chane as being a man to mistreat women, white or red. Slack was vicious, but under control of McPherson. It narrowed down to Manrube.

This individual swaggered into the camp circle. He had stretched two ropes on Panquitch, in opposite directions, and for the time being the great stallion was tractable. Manrube's blond face showed heat, not all of excitement. He shot a malignant glance at Chane, and leered. The true nature of the man came out when he was on the side in control. As he turned to look Sue up and down, Chane saw the surge of blood ridge his neck. Chane also saw a whiskey flask in his hip pocket and a gun in his belt.

"Bud, I heard you weren't boss of your outfit," said Chane, whose wits were active.

"Huh! The hell you did. When an' whar did you hear thet?"

"Reckon it was in Wund, when we drove Melberne's horses in."

"Wal, you heerd wrong," replied McPherson, gruffly, and his glance fell on Manrube with a glint that surely fanned a flame of cunning in Chane's mind.

"Bud, I trapped Panquitch in a deep hole down in the canyon," went on Chane. "It was a dirty trick to play on such a horse. I roped him. We had an awful time. He nearly drowned Brutus and me. But we got him out. And then—what do you think?"

"I've no idea, Weymer," returned the outlaw, eagerly. He had the true rider's love for a horse, the true wrangler's ambition and pride. Only adverse circumstances had made him a thief. Chane knew how to work on his feelings.

"Bud, I let Panquitch go free!" declared Chane, impressively.

"Aw, now, Weymer, you can't expect me to believe thet," said McPherson, with a broad smile.

"I swear it's true."

"But you're a wild-hoss wrangler. I've heerd of you for years," declared the outlaw, incredulously.

"I was. But no more. Bud, I'm giving it to you straight. Panquitch was the last wild horse I'll ever rope. I let him go free."

"But what fer? You darned loco liar!" shouted McPherson, getting red in the face.

"Ask Sue Melberne," replied Chane, recognizing the moment to impress the outlaw. He was intensely interested, curious, doubtful, yet fascinated. He turned to Sue. She was pale, yet composed, and aside from the heaving of her bosom, showed no agitation.

"Girl, what's he givin' me? Guff?"

"No, it's perfectly true. He let Panquitch go. I watched him do it."

"So did I," spoke up Chess, in a loud voice. "He and Sue were out of their heads. They let Panquitch go!"

"Wal, I'll be damned!" ejaculated McPherson. "Shore, girl, I don't see any reason for you to lie about a hoss, even Panquitch. But I gotta know why, if you want me to believe."

"It was my fault," replied Sue, deliberately. "I told Chane—if he'd free Panquitch—I'd be his wife."

"An' he took you up," shouted McPherson, in gleeful wonder.

"Yes. He let me pull the lasso free."

"Wal, I've seen the day I could have done the same, even if it had been Panquitch," boomed McPherson. From the rough, hardened outlaw that speech was a subtle compliment to both Sue and Chane. It hinted, also, of a time when McPherson had not been what he was now. Suddenly he lost that shadow of memory, and wheeled to Manrube, who stood derisive and rancorous, glaring at Chane.

"Didn't I tell you that hoss was tuckered out? Didn't I say he was all wet?"

"Yes, you said so, but I don't have to believe you. And Weymer's a liar," retorted Manrube.

"Sure I'm a liar—when you've got a gun and I haven't," interposed Chane, stingingly.

"Huh! You wouldn't call the little lady a liar, too, would you?" demanded McPherson.

"She would lie and he would swear to it," snapped Manrube.

"Wal, that's no matter, except where I come from men didn't call girls' names. But what I gotta beat into your thick head is this, that Panquitch was a spent horse. An' you never seen it. You thought you roped him when he was good as ever. You never *seen* it!"

"Suppose I didn't," returned Manrube, furiously. "I roped him, spent or not. And he's mine."

"Hell! You're a fine wild-hoss wrangler!" exclaimed McPherson, in disgust. "You don't even get my hunch. Let me say it slow an' plain. In this heah Utah there's a code, the same among hoss thieves as among wranglers. It's love of a grand hoss. An' I'm tellin' you it's a damn shame Panquitch fell into your rope."

"Say, Bud, are you going to let Manrube keep that horse?" demanded Chane, ringingly, sure now of his game. He could play upon this outlaw's feelings as upon an instrument.

"Whaat?" queried McPherson, as if staggered. The idea Chane launched had struck like a thunderbolt.

"If it's your outfit—if you're the boss, Panquitch is yours," asserted Chane, positively. "That's the law of the range. But even if it wasn't would you let Manrube keep that grand stallion? He'll ruin the horse. He couldn't break him. He couldn't ride him. For this man is not the real thing as a rider. He never was a wrangler...Now, McPherson, listen. You may be a horse thief, but you're a real rider. You have a rider's love for a grand stallion like Panquitch. You have a wrangler's pride in him. You'd never beat Panquitch, now would you?"

"Hell no! I never beat any hoss," shouted the outlaw, hoarsely.

"There you are," announced Chane, with finality, and he threw up his hands. How well he knew the state into which he had thrown McPherson. Chane actually thrilled in the suspense of the issue at stake. His argument had been sound, his persuasion hard for a rider to resist, but he staked most on McPherson's dislike of Manrube. Any honest rider would despise Manrube, but McPherson, hard, strong, matured outlaw, who, bad as he was, would have died for a horse, would hate him.

"Reckon you're talkin' fine, Weymer, but ain't a little of it fer your hoss Brutus?" queried McPherson shrewdly.

"No, I never thought of my horse. But now

you mention him, I'll say this. You stole my last bunch of mustangs. Brutus is all I have left. A horse and a saddle! That's the extent of my riches. You'd not be so mean as to rob me of them?"

"Wal, Weymer, I reckon I wouldn't now," he replied, significantly. "Brutus ain't so bad. But what'd I do with him now? Haw! Haw!"

Chane drew a quick breath of relief, yet the suspense of that argument was in no wise diminished.

Manrube grew black with rage. His light eyes gleamed balefully.

"Bud McPherson, you mean you'll take Panquitch?" he rasped out

"Wal, you heerd Weymer's idee of the code of the range," replied the outlaw, calmly. With all his acumen and experience he had no fear of Manrube. Rather contempt!

"Code be damned!" yelled Manrube, fiercely. "Panquitch is mine. I roped him."

"Shore. But you're in my outfit, an' what you ketch is mine, if I want it. An' I want Panquitch. Savvy?"

Chane, watching so piercingly, saw a break in Manrube's quivering rage. His body grew rigid before the blackness left his face. If Chane had been in McPherson's boots he would have reacted with subtle keeness to those peculiar changes.

"You're a horse thief," panted Manrube, suddenly crouching.

"Wal, wal, wal!" guffawed McPherson, and he bent double with the mirth of the joke.

When he straightened up it was to meet the red flame and the blue spurt of Manrube's gun. He uttered a gasp and fell limply, as if his legs had been chopped from under him.

Manrube did not lower the leveled gun. Smoke issued from the dark hole in the barrel. All the men seemed paralyzed, except Chane, who stepped aside, with eyes roving for a weapon in the belts near him. But none showed. Chane read Manrube's ferocious face. It was now gray and set with murderous intent.

"Step aside, Slack, or I'll kill you," he hissed. "I want Weymer."

Slack frantically leaped aside, leaving Chane exposed. But Manrube did not fire. The smoking gun shook in his nerveless hand, and fell. At that instant, perhaps a fraction of a second before, Chane heard a tiny spat. He knew what it was. A lead bullet striking flesh!

Chane's gaze shot over Manrube's outstretched hand to his face. It was the same, but fixed. Then from the ragged brushy cliff above rang out the crack of a rifle. The echoes clapped back and forth. Over Manrube's glazed blank eyes, in his forehead, appeared a little round hole, first blue, then red. He swayed and fell, full length, face down.

This action was incredibly swift. Before Chane could make a move to rush to Sue he heard another spat. The bullet spanged off bone. Slack was knocked flat. Again the sharp crack of a rifle rang out. It broke the rigidity of that group. Frantically the three left of

McPherson's band rushed for their horses. Slack leaped up, bloody of face, wild of mien, and he bellowed:

"It's them hell-bound Piutes! Bud swore they was trailin' us. Get on an' ride!"

Not far behind was he in a leap to the saddle. The horses plunged madly and broke up the canyon. Another shot sounded from the cliff, deadened by the trampling hoofs. Then the swiftly moving dark blot of riders disappeared.

Chane's first thought was for Sue. He ran to her, took her in his arms. She seemed stiff, but her hands suddenly clutched him. Her cheek, which was all he could see as he grasped her, was ashen in hue.

"Come away, Sue, dear," he said, gently, half-carrying her. "Over here where Chess is ... You're safe. I'm all right. We're all saved. They went up a different canyon from the one your father took. They won't meet him."

Sue hid her face against his breast while a long shudder went through her.

"How terrible." she whispered, hoarsely. "All so—so sudden! Let me sit down. I'm weak and sick. But I won't faint."

"Sure you won't. Just keep your eyes away—from over there," replied Chane, and releasing her he ran to untie Chess's bonds.

"My Gawd! What blew in here?" cried Chess, in decidedly weak voice.

"Kinda stormy and smoky, wasn't it, boy," replied Chane. "I've seen some of that sort of thing. Been in it too ... You go to Sue and talk. Get her mind off it."

Chane's next move was to release Lough-bridge, who sat up with popping eyes and incoherent speech. From him Chane ran to the dead men, who had fallen close to each other. He covered them with canvas. After that Chane gazed up at the cliff whence had come the rifle shots. Thin clouds of blue smoke were floating on the still air, gradually thinning. The cliff was broken and ragged, green with brush, and marked by a wildness of ledge up to the rim. It was not far to the top. Full well Chane knew who had fired that shot fatal to Manrube. But he would never tell, and no one else would ever know. Toddy Nokin had paid his debt in a way only Chane full understood. He hurried back to Sue, finding her recovered, though she was leaning on Chess's shoulder. Chane promptly relieved him of the burden.

"Humph! I thought she was in the family now," protested Chess.

"Boy, you wander in mind," returned Chane, softly.

"If only Dad would come." exclaimed Sue, in anxious dread.

"Well, he's coming," said Chane, gladly. "Look up the canyon. Did you ever see your Dad run like that? He's scared Sue, either for himself or us."

Sue gave vent to a smothered sob of relief and then broke down.

Melberne amused Chane, and appeared to be a fascinating object to Chess. The leader of the outfit had returned out of breath, and if Chane was any judge of men, both frightened and furious. When he caught his breath he blurted out many queries, but vouchsafed no information about himself. Chane's observant eye, however, noted Melberne's skinned and bruised wrists, and how conscious he was of them, a circumstance undoubtedly due to pain.

But McPherson had lied to Chane. The outlaws had happened to run into Melberne and had tied him up. Chane grew more convinced of this as the moments passed. Besides Melberne's telltale wrists, which he had probably skinned by working free of a tight rope, he had come back minus his gun. Moreover, his relief at the sight of Sue safe and well, though pale, was so great as to approach collapse. Lastly, when Chane had pulled aside the canvas to expose Manrube and McPherson, lying so ghastly and suggestive, he had cursed them under his breath.

But the amusing part of this sequence was the argument between Melberne and Loughbridge, and Chess's deep concern.

"I'm sorry, Jim, you shore have queered yourself with me," declared Melberne for at least the tenth time. His demeanor, however, was not in harmony with his hard words. He strode to and fro nervously, as was his wont when perturbed.

"But, Mel, this here Manrube made a damn fool of you, same as me," persisted Loughbridge.

"Shore, I acknowledge that. But he didn't make me double-cross you."

"I didn't. You ain't far. We couldn't agree,

about money mostly, an' you fired me out of your outfit. I leave it to Chess, here. You ain't jest fair."

"Boss, if you'll excuse me, I think it was more temper with you than justice," replied Chess, with immense gravity.

"Hugh! Wal, I'll be darned!" quoth Melberne, surveying the boy in great disfavor. "I reckon you'd like to see Loughbridge homestead with us over there at Nightwatch Spring."

"That'd be fair and square of you," returned Chess, losing his dignity of a judge.

"An' fetch Ora along to live with him, huh?" went on Melberne, ironically.

"I should smile," answered Chess, with an anticlimax of weakness.

"See heah, young man, you've got good stuff, but you talk too much. I've a mind to fire you."

"Aw, now—boss," yapped Chess, abjectly.

"Wal, if you don't marry Ora before spring I will fire you," growled Melberne.

Then he turned to his former partner. "Jim, I reckon I've no call to crow over you. I've had my lesson. An' if you've had yours, mebbe we'll both profit by it. My fault is temper, an' yours is a little too much fondness for money... Let's begin over again, each for himself. It's a new country. You're welcome to homestead in my canyon. There's room for another rancher. Some day before long there'll be a settlement west of Wund. An' that'll make our problem easier."

Panquitch startled Chane, and all the others, with one of his ringing neighs; and with head, ears, and mane erect he faced up the canyon.

Shrill whistles answered him. Chane espied a troop of wild horses coming out of the shadow.

"By golly! there's Panquitch's band," said Chane, pointing. "They're looking for him. They'll pass us. Everybody lie low."

Chane crouched behind a rock with Sue, who whispered that Panquitch should be free to go with them. It did seem to Chane that the straining stallion would free himself from Manrube's ropes. For some moments the wild horses could not be seen, owing to the fact that Chane and Sue were low down. At last, however, they came in sight, trotting cautiously, wary as always, but not yet having caught scent of the camp. Only a faint breeze stirred and that came down the canyon. The whistling of Panquitch must have been a factor in their cautious approach. At the junction of the canyons the space was fully a hundred yards wide, and owing to the stream bed, somewhat lower on the side opposite the camp. The wild-horse band worked down this side, trotting, with heads erect until they caught scent of the camp, then burst into headlong flight, and in a dusty cloud, with a clattering roar they sped by, and down the canyon to disappear.

"Sue, wasn't it great?" queried Chane, as he got up.

But Sue had not been looking at the fleet

band of wild horses; her startled gaze was fixed on Panquitch.

"Oh, Chane, look! He's broken one of the ropes!" cried Sue.

Chane wheeled in time to see the remnant of broken lasso fall off the superb tawny shoulders. The other lasso was round the noble arched neck of the stallin and had now become taut. Panquitch reared and lunged back with all his weight. As luck would have it, the rope broke at the noose. The stallion fell heavily, then raised on his forefeet, with mouth open. The broken noose hung loose. He was not yet sure of freedom.

Chess broke the silence with a wailing, "Oh, the ropes were rotten. They broke. He'll get away. Gimme a rope, a rope! A rope!"

"Boy, keep still," shouted Chane, sternly. "Can't you see Panquitch was never born to be roped?"

The stallion painfully got to his feet. As the broken noose slipped from his neck he jumped as if stung. Then he walked through camp. He shied at the canvas covering the dead men, and breaking into a trot, he headed down the canyon.

"Wal, I cain't pretend to savvy you, Chane," observed Melberne, scratching his head in his perplexity. "But shore I will say this. Somehow I'm glad you let him go."

"Damn it! So'm I!" yelled Chess, suddenly red of face, as if he had been unjustly accused. "But I—I was so crazy to keep him!"

Chane turned to Sue with a smile.

"He's gone, my dear. Suppose we ride down

to the slope where he'll climb up the mesa.
There's work to do here that I'd rather you
didn't see."

Melberne approved of that idea for Sue.
"An' when you come back we'll be packed to
change camp."

Not until Sue had ridden at quite a brisk
trot, keeping up with Brutus, all the way down
to the oval break in the canyon, did her blood
warm and beat out the dark blot of horror in
her mind.

But at the foot of the beautiful slope of wavy
rock all that turgid emotion fell away from
her, as if it had never been. She had grown
weak, but now she was strong. The purple
heights above, gold-rimmed under the sun,
inspired her as before, only now with something added to the wild joy of freedom.

"Follow me close, sweetheart," called
Chane. "I see Panquitch far above. If we hurry
we can reach the top and watch him climb the
mesa."

"Ah, Chane, you'll never lose me now, on
any kind of trails," called Sue, in reply, and
urged her horse close to Brutus.

To and fro, across and around, up and
down, far to this side, and back to the other,
onward and upward they rode over the
smooth waves and hollows of red sandstone.
As they climbed, the purple and amber lights
grew brighter, and the shadows of the canyon
below grew deeper. They reached the zone of
cream and yellow rock, crumbling like baked
clay under the hoofs of the horses. Out of the

dark depths they rose to the sunset-flushed heights.

"Oh, where is Panquitch?" Sue kept calling. But he had always just gone over a wave of rock.

All above the corrugated world of wind-torn stone streamed fan-shaped bars and bands of light, centering toward and disappearing over the height of ridge they had almost attained. Broken massed clouds floated in the west, dark-purple, silver-rimmed, golden-edged, in a sea of azure blue. The lights of sunset were intensifying. Sue felt that she rode up the last curved wave of an opal sea. She saw Chane shade his eyes from the fire of the sun. Like a god of the riders he seemed to her, bareheaded, his face alight, his sharp profile against the background of gold. Then she mounted to Chane's side, and it was as if in one step she had surmounted a peak.

All the forces of nature seemed to have united in one grand spectacle the rugged canyon country of colored rock waved level with the setting sun, and above it, from west to north, loomed the cloud-piercing bulk of Wild Horse Mesa.

"Panquitch! I see him, Sue," said Chane, his voice ringing deep. "He's all alone. His band has gone up. Look! The fold in the wall! It could never be seen except when the sun shines as now. What a trail! Even the Piutes do not know it. Hard smooth rock over the bench, and then the zigzag up that crack. See, he shines gold and black in the sun!"

At last Sue's straining gaze was rewarded by clear sight of Panquitch climbing, apparently the very wall of the mesa. With bated breath Sue watched him, conscious of more in the moment than just the climbing freedom of a wild horse. But it was beyond her. It led her thoughts beyond emotions, deep into the dim past of her inheritance. But she had loved Panquitch or some creature like him in a world before this.

The intense flare of gold changed as the sun began to sink behind cloud and rim. It yielded to the wondrous lilac haze. Sue cried out in a transport. Panquitch, too, seemed less a wild horse, more of an unreal creature, giving life to the grandeur and desolation of the naked rock-ribs of the earth.

"He's almost on top," said Chane, joyfully. He clung to the physical thing—to the flesh and blood Panquitch, to his pursuit and capture and release, to his recapture and escape, to the long winding mysterious and hidden trail in and out of the canyons, to the wonderful wall of Wild Horse Mesa.

Sue felt all these, deeply, poignantly, but beyond them inexplicable and vague, was the spiritual thing Panquitch typified. She endowed him with soul. She had gazed at him, recognizing in him something within herself.

Panquitch came out on top of the rim, sharply silhouetted against the blue sky, and stood a moment looking down, with his long mane and tail streaming in the wind. The lilac gaze lent him unreality, but the uplift of his head gave him life. Wild and grand he seemed to Sue, fitting that last stand of wild horses. He moved against the sky; he was gone.

"Oh, Panquitch, stay up there always!" called Sue.

Chane smiled upon her. "Sweetheart, I'd stake my life he'll never feel another rope."

"We alone know his trail to the heights. And we never will tell?"

"Never, Sue."

"You will not show dad how to get on top of Wild Horse Mesa?" she begged. "So he could run sheep and cattle up there?"

"I promise, Sue. Why, do you imagine I could ever become that much of a rancher? It may be long before another rider, or an Indian, happens on this secret. Maybe never. Some distant day airships might land on Wild Horse Mesa. But what if they do? An hour of curiosity, an achievement to boast of—then gone! Wild Horse Mesa rises even above this world of rock. It was meant for eagles, wild horses—and for lonely souls like mine."

Slowly the transformation of sunset worked its miracles of evanescent change and exquisite color. Gold and silver fire faded, died away. The sun sank below the verge. And from out of the depths where it had gone rose the afterglow, deepening the lilac haze to purple.

"Chane, you have made Wild Horse Mesa yours," said Sue. "Millions of men can never take it from you. As for me—Panquitch seems mine. He's like my heart or something in my blood."

"Yes, I think I understand you," he replied, dreamily. "We must labor—we must live as people have lived before. But these thoughts are beautiful. You are Panquitch and I am Wild Horse Mesa."

JUNGLE RIVER

Some of Zane Grey's true life adventures are fully as exciting as those he depicted in his novels. This one tells of he and his guides going by primitive boats down an unknown jungle river full of rapids, ticks, leeches, snakes, and not the least of the hazards encountered—giant crocodiles.

That night my dreams were not pleasant. I awoke from one in a fright and had no small task to persuade myself that half of my anatomy had not been chewed off by huge crawling black things.

It must have been late in the night, for the moon was low, and I was falling asleep again when the clink of tin pans made me sit up with a start. Some animal was prowling about camp. I peered into the moonlight shadows, but could make out no unfamiliar object. Still I was not satisfied, so I awoke Pepe and told him to get up and help me chase away the night marauders.

Certainly it was not my intention to let Pepe get out ahead of me and to take any possible risks; nevertheless, I was tired and slow, and Pepe rolled out of the tent before I had started.

"Santa Maria!" he shrieked.

I fumbled under my pillow for a gun, George raised up so quickly that he bumped my head, making me see a million stars.

From outside came a slithery, rustling noise, then another yell that was deadened by a sounding splash. I leaped out with my gun, George at my elbow. Pepe stood just back of the tent, his arms upraised, and he appeared stunned. The water near the bank was boiling and bubbling; waves were dashing on the shore, and ripples spreading in a circle.

"Alligator!" I exclaimed, before Pepe had time to speak.

"Si, si, Senor," replied he, and his big hands trembled. Then he said that when he stepped out of the tent the alligator was right in camp, not ten feet from where we lay. He also said that these brutes were man-eaters and that he would watch the rest of the night. I thought him, like all the natives, inclined to exaggerate; however, I made no objection to his holding watch. Nothing further happened to disturb our rest.

In the morning when I got up I viewed my body with curiosity. The ticks and the cigarettes had left me a beautifully tattooed specimen of aborigine. My body, especially my arms, bore hundreds of little reddish scars—bites and burns together. There was not, however, any itching or irritation, for which I made sure I had to thank Pepe's skill and the *canu*.

George did not get up when I called him. Thinking his sleep might have been broken, I let him alone a while longer, but when breakfast was smoking I gave him a prod. He rolled over, looking haggard and glum.

"I'm sick," he said.

My cheerfulness left me, for I knew what sickness or injury did to a camping trip. George complained of aching bones, headache, and cramps, and showed a tongue with a yellow coating. I said he had eaten too much fresh meat, but Pepe, after seeing George vomit, called it a name that sounded like "colenturus."

"What's that?" I inquired.

"Tropic fever," replied George. "I've had it before."

For awhile he was a very sick boy. I had a little medicine case, and from it I administered what I thought was best, and he grew easier presently and went to sleep. Then I dispatched Pepe to the bamboo swale to get my coat, while I sat down to deliberate on the situation.

Whatever way I viewed it, I always came back to the same thing—we must get out of the jungle, and as we could not go back, we must go on down the river and trust to luck. That was a bad enough proposition even if George had been well. It was then I had a subtle change of feeling; a shade of gloom seemed to pervade my spirit.

Pepe returned with my coat, and also a choice collection of ticks. He reported big jaguar tracks around the remains of the deer carcass I had left in the swale. If George had not required my attention I would have had another watch in the twilight. I stayed in camp and had the satisfaction of seeing him very much better by bedtime. I forbade him, and Pepe too, to drink any more unboiled water. In the morning George was well enough to walk; however, he appeared weak and shaky. I decided to break camp immediately.

By nine o'clock we were packed, and turning into the shady channel, soon were out in the sunlight and saying good-bye to Cypress Island. At the moment I did not feel sorry to go, yet I knew that reaction would come to me by and by, and that Cypress Island would take its place in my memory as one more haunting, calling, wild place.

We turned a curve to run under a rocky bluff from which came a muffled roar of rapids. A long projecting point of rock extended across the river, allowing the water to rush by only at a narrow mill-race channel close to the shore. It was a ticklish obstacle to get around. There was no possibility of lifting the boat over the bridge of rock, and the alternative was shooting the channel.

We got out upon the rocks, only to find that drifting the boat around the sharp point was out of the question, owing to a dangerously swift current. I tried the depth of the water—about four feet. Then I dragged the boat back a little distance and stepped into the river.

"Look! Look!" cried Pepe, pointing to the bank.

About ten yards away was a bare shelf of mud, glistening with water and showing the deep tracks of an alligator. It was a slide and manifestly had just been vacated. The alligator tracks resembled the imprint of a giant's hand.

"Come out!" yelled George, and Pepe jabbered to his saints.

"We've got to go down this river," I replied, and I kept on wading till I got the boat in the current. I was frightened, of course, but I kept on despite that. The boat lurched into the channel, stern first, and I leaped up on the bow. We shot down with tremendous speed, and the boat whirled before I could scramble to the oars. What was worse, an overhanging tree with dead snags left scarce room to pass beneath. I ducked to prevent being swept overboard, but one of the snags lifted me into the air. I grasped at the first thing I could lay hands on, which happened to be a box, but I could not hold to it because the boat threatened to go on, leaving me kicking in midair, holding up a box of potatoes. I clutched a gunwale, only to see the water swell dangerously over the edge. In angry impotence I loosened my hold. Then the snag broke, just in the nick of time, for in a second more the boat would have swept away from me. I fell across the bow, held on, and soon, to my satisfaction, drifted from under the threshing branches, where I got to the oars. Pepe and George walked round the ledge, and were all smiles when they reached me.

"Boys, it wasn't funny," I declared, soberly.

"I said it was coming to us," replied George, with a hint of his old humor.

There were rapids below, which I went at in the way men face obstacles in the wilderness, when the dominant and controlling thought is to get out. More than one high wave curled spitefully round Pepe's shoulders. We came to a fall where the river dropped a few feet straight down. As usual in such places, I sent the boys around to meet me below. George made a detour and Pepe jumped right off the ledge into a foot or more of water.

Used as I was becoming to Pepe's wild yell, the one he now pealed out sent a shiver over me. Before looking, I snatched my rifle from the boat, then leaped upon the ledge of rock.

Pepe appeared to be sailing out into the pool, but his feet were not moving. I had only an instant, but in that I saw under Pepe a long black swimming shape leaving a wake in the water. He had stepped upon an alligator. Suddenly he leaped to a dry stone, and the energy of his leap carried him into the river beyond. Like a flash he was out again, spouting water. I shot a magazine of shells at the alligator. He made a thunderous surge, churning up a slimy foam, then vanished in a pool.

"I guess it's alligator day," I said, changing the clip in my rifle. "I'll bet I made a hole in that one. Look out below, boys."

I shoved the boat over the ledge in line with Pepe, and it floated to him, while I picked my way around the rocky shore. We piled aboard again and proceeded on our journey. I cautioned the boys to avoid wading unless it was impossible, in which case to use care where

228

they stepped. Pepe pointed now and then to huge bubbles breaking on the surface of the water, with the information that they were made by alligators.

From then on my hands were full. We struck swift water, where rapid after rapid, fall on fall, took us downhill at a rate that was grim gratification to me. Where the current was not rough, it yet had a five or six-mile speed, and as we had no portages, and pounded through the corrugated rapids of big waves, we made by far the best time of the voyage. The hot hours passed, cool for us because we were always wet; the sun sank behind a bald hill; the wind ceased to whip the streamers of moss; and at last, in a gathering twilight, we halted at a wide, flat rock to make camp.

"Forty miles, if we made an inch!" I declared, and both the boys said more.

We built a fire, cooked our supper, and then, weary and silent, rolled into our blankets. Next morning the mists had not lifted from the river when we shoved off, determined to beat the record of yesterday. Difficulties beset us from the start: the highest waterfall of our trip; a leak in the boat; deep, short rapids; narrows with choppy waves; a whirlpool where we turned round and round, seemingly unable to row out. Nor did we get out till Pepe lassoed a snag and pulled us out.

About noon we came to another narrow chute brawling down into a deep, foamy pool. Again I sent the boys around and backed the boat through. Either I was tired or careless, for I drifted too close to a half-submerged rock, and try as I might, at the last moment I could not avoid a collision. As the stern went hard at the rock I expected to break something, but was surprised at the soft thud with which I struck. It flashed into my mind that the rock was moss-covered. Quick as the thought followed a rumble under the boat, the stern heaved up; there was a great sheet-like splash, and then a blow that splintered the gunwale. The boat shunted off, affording me a good view of a very angry, eight-foot alligator. I had a clear view of him at close range. Manifestly he had been sleeping on the rock when I disturbed him. It was this look at him that enabled me to make a discovery. Instead of the wide rounded nose of the alligator he had the sharp nose and narrow jaws of the crocodile.

"Hey, George, that was a crocodile!" I shouted. "These devils are not alligators at all—they're crocodiles!"

"Same thing," replied George, laconically.

"Well, my boy, not so you'd notice it," I added. "I'll tell you something...."

"Say, the boat's half-full of water; the gunwale's all split up," interrupted he.

We unloaded, turned out the water, broke up a box to use for repairs, and mended the damaged gunwale—work that lost us more than a good hour. Once more under way, we made some interesting observations. The river ceased to stand on end in places; crocodiles slipped off of every muddy promontory, and wide trails ridged the steep clay banks.

"Cattle trails, Pepe says," remarked George. "Wild cattle roam all over the jungles along the Panuco."

It was a well known fact that the rancheros of Tamaulipas State had no idea how many cattle they owned. I was so eager to see if Pepe had been correct that I went ashore, to find the trails were indeed those of cattle.

"Then, Pepe, we must be somewhere near the Panuco River," I said.

"*Quien sabe*," rejoined he, quietly.

When we rounded the next curve we came upon a herd of cattle. They clattered up the bank, raising a cloud of dust.

"Wilder than deer," I exclaimed.

From that point conditions along the river changed. The banks were no longer green; the beautiful cypresses gave place to other trees, as huge, as moss-wound, but more rugged and of gaunt outline; the flowers and vines and shady nooks disappeared. Everywhere wild, wide-horned steers and cows plunged up the banks. Everywhere buzzards rose from gruesome feasts. The shore was lined with dead cattle and the stench of putrefying flesh was almost unbearable. We passed cattle mired in the mud, being slowly tortured to death by flies and hunger; we passed cattle that had slipped off steep banks and could not get back, and were bellowing dismally; and also we passed strangely acting cattle that Pepe said had gone crazy from ticks in their ears. I would have put these miserable beasts out of their misery had not George restrained me with a few words about Mexican law.

With all this I sickened, and though I drove the feeling from me, it continually returned. George lay flat on the canvas, shaded with a couple of palm leaves; Pepe rowed on and on, growing more and more into a settled quiet. His quick, responsive smile was wanting now. By way of a diversion, and also in the hope of securing a skin, I began to shoot at the crocodiles. George came out of his lethargy and took up his rifle. He would have had to be ill indeed to forswear any possible shooting; and now that I had removed the bar, he forgot he had fever. Every hundred yards or so we would come upon a crocodile, measuring somewhere from six feet on, and occasionally we would see a great yellow one, as large as a log. Seldom did we get within good range of these huge fellows, and shooting from a moving boat was not easy. The smaller ones, however, allowed us to approach quite close. George bounced many a thirty-two bullet off the bank, but he never hit a crocodile. I allowed him to have the shots, for the fun of it, and besides, I was watching for a big one.

"George, that rifle of yours is loaded. It doesn't shoot where you aim."

When we got unusually close to a small crocodile George verified my statement by missing his game by some yards. He promptly threw the worn-out rifle overboard, an act that caused Pepe much concern.

Thereupon I proceeded to try my luck. Instructing Pepe to row about in the middle of the stream, I kept my eye on one shore, while

George watched the other. Since my failure to kill the jaguar I had lost faith in the little automatic, and now I had a chance to find out what it really could do. I shot half a dozen small crocodiles, but they slipped off the bank before we could get ashore. This did not appear to be the fault of the rifle, for some of the reptiles were shot almost in two pieces. But I had yet to learn more about the tenacity of life of these water brutes. Several held still long enough for me to shoot them through, then with a plunge they went into the water, sinking at once in a bloody foam. I knew the bullets had penetrated, for we found large holes in the mud banks lined with bits of bloody skin and bone.

"There's one," said George, pointing. "Let's get closer, so we can grab him. He's got a good piece to go before he reaches water."

Pepe rolled slowly along, guiding the boat a little nearer the shore. At forty feet the crocodile raised himself, standing on his short legs so that all but his tail was free of the ground. He opened his huge jaws, either in astonishment or to intimidate us, I imagined, and then I shot him straight down the throat. He flopped convulsively and started to slide and roll. When he reached the water he turned over on his back with his feet sticking up, resembling a huge frog. Pepe rowed hard to the shore, just as the crocodile, with one last convulsion, rolled off into deeper water. I reached over, grasped his foot, and was drawing him up when a sight of cold, glassy eyes and open fanged jaws made me let go. Then he sank in water where we could not touch bottom with an oar.

"Let's get one if it takes a week," declared George. The lad might be sick, but there was nothing wrong with his spirit. "Gee! Look there!" he exclaimed. "Oh, I guess it's a log. Too big!"

We had often been unable to tell the difference between a crocodile and a log of driftwood until it was too late. In this instance a long, dirty gray object lay upon a low bank. Despite its immense size, which certainly made the chances in favor of its being a log, I determined this time to be fooled on the right side. I had seen a dozen logs—as I thought— suddenly become animated and slip into the river.

"Hold steady, Pepe. I'll take a crack at that, just for luck."

The distance was about a hundred yards, a fine range for the little rifle. Resting on my knee, I sighted low, under the gray object, and pulled the trigger twice. There were two spats so close together as to be barely distinguishable. The log of driftwood leaped to life.

"It's a crocodile!" yelled George. "You hit— you hit! Gee! Will you listen to that?"

"Row hard, Pepe—pull!"

He bent to the oars and the boat flew shoreward.

The huge crocodile, opening yard-long jaws, snapped them shut with loud cracks. Then he beat the bank with his tail. It was as limber as a willow, but he seemed unable to move his central parts, his thick bulk where I had sent the two mushroom bullets. Whack! Whack! Whack! The sodden blows jarred pieces from the clay bank above him. Each blow was powerful enough to have stove in the planking of a ship. All at once he lunged upward and, falling over backward, slid down his runway into a few inches of water, where he stuck.

"Go in above him, Pepe," I shouted. "Here! What a monster!"

Deliberately, at scarce twenty feet, I shot the remaining four shells into the crocodile. The bullets tore through his horny hide and spouted up blood and muddy water. The terrible lashing tail swung back and forth almost too swiftly for the eye to catch. A deluge of mud and water descended upon us and weighed down the boat. George and I jumped out upon the bank to escape it. There we ran to and fro in aimless excitement. I still clutched my rifle, but I had no shells for it. George was absurd enough to fling a stone into the blood-tinged cloud of muddy froth and spray that hid the thrashing leviathan. Presently the commotion subsided enough for us to see the great crocodile lying half on his back with belly all torn and bloody, and huge clawlike hands pawing the air. He was edging, slipping off into deeper water.

"He'll get away! He'll get away!" cried George. "What'll we do?" I racked my brains and suddenly had an inspiration. Pepe snatched up his lariat and, without waiting to coil it, cast the loop. He caught one of the flippers, hauled tight on it, just as the crocodile slipped out of sight off the muddy ledge. George and I ran to the boat and, grasping hold of the lasso with Pepe, we squared away and began to pull. Plain it was that the crocodile was not coming up so easily. We could not budge him.

"Hang on, boys!" I shouted. "It's a tug of war."

The lasso suddenly streaked out with a kind of twang. Crash! went Pepe into the bottom of the boat. I went sprawling into the mud, and George, who had the last hold, went to his knees, but valiantly clung to the slipping rope. Bounding up, I grasped it from him and wound it round the sharp nose of the bowsprit.

"Get in! Hustle!" I called, falling aboard. "You're always saying it's coming to us. Here's where!"

George had hardly got into the boat when the crocodile pulled us off shore, and away we went, sailing downstream.

"Whoop! All aboard for Panuco!" yelled George.

"Now, Pepe, you don't need to row any more—we've a water horse," I added.

But Pepe did not enter into the spirit of the occasion. He kept calling on the saints and crying, *Mucha malo*. George and I, however, were hilarious. We had not yet had experience enough to know crocodiles.

Faster and faster we went. The water began to surge away from the bow and leave a gurgling wake behind the stern. Soon we reached the middle of the river, where the water was deepest, and the lasso went almost straight down.

I felt the stern of the boat gradually lifted, and then, in alarm, I saw the front end sinking in the water. The crocodile was hauling the bow under.

"Pepe—your machete! Cut the lasso!" I ordered, sharply.

Wildly Pepe searched under the seat and along the gunwales. He could not find the machete.

"Cut the rope!" I thundered. "Use a knife, the ax—anything—only cut it, cut it quick!"

Pepe could find nothing. Knife in hand, I leaped over his head, sprawled headlong over the trunk, and slashed the taut lasso just as the water began to roar into the boat. The bow bobbed up as a cork that had been under. But we had shipped six inches of water.

"Row ashore, Pepe. Steady there. Trim the boat, George."

We beached on a hard clay bank, and rested a little before unloading to turn out the water.

"*Grande!*" observed Pepe.

"Yes, he was big," I assented.

"I wonder what's going to happen to us next," added George.

Pepe's long years of *mozo* work rowing for the tarpon fishermen now stood us in good stead. All the hot hours of the day he bent steadily to the oars. Occasionally we came to rifts, but they presented no difficulty to our passage, being merely swift, shallow channels over sandy or gravelly bottom. The rocks and the rapids were things of the past.

What annoyed us now was the scarcity of camping sites. The muddy margins of the river, the steep banks, and the tick-infested forests offered few places where it was possible to rest, to say nothing of sleep. Every turn in the widening river gave us hope, which resulted in disappointment. We found consolation, however, in the fact that every turn and every hour put us so much farther on our way. About five o'clock we had unexpected good fortune in the shape of a small sand bar, cut off from the mainland, and therefore free of cattle tracks. It was clean and dry, with a pile of driftwood at one end. Here we pitched camp.

But for the sense of foreboding in my mind, the vague feeling that all was not well with us, that we should hurry, hurry, hurry, I should have recovered my former cheerful spirits. George seemed to be holding his own, and Pepe's brooding quiet had at least grown no more noticeable, still I could not rid myself of a shade of gloom. If I had answered the question that knocked at my mind, instead of fighting it off, I should have admitted the certainty of disaster. So I kept myself busy at all kinds of tasks, and when there were no more for that day I watched the flight of wild fowl.

The farther down the river we travelled, the more numerous were the ducks and herons and cranes. But I saw no more of the beautiful *Pato Real*, as Pepe called them, or the little russet-colored ducks, or the dismal-voiced bitterns. On the other hand, wild geese and canvas-backs had become common and there were flocks of teal.

Pepe cooked duck, as usual, but George had lost his taste for meat and I made a frugal meal of rice. "Boys, the less you eat from now on, the better for you." It took resolution to drink the cocoa, for I could not banish thought of the green water and the shore line of dead and decaying cattle. Still, I was parched with thirst; I had to drink. That night we slept ten hours without turning over. Next morning I had to shake Pepe to rouse him.

I took turns at the oars with Pepe. It was not only that I fancied he was weakening and in need of an occasional rest, but the fact that I wanted to be occupied, and especially to keep in good condition. We made thirty miles by four o'clock, and most of it against a breeze. Not in the whole distance did we pass half a dozen places fit for a camp. Toward evening the river narrowed again, resembling somewhat the Santa Rosa of our earlier acquaintance. The magnificent dark forests crowded high on the banks, always screened and curtained by gray moss, as if to keep their secrets.

The sun was just tipping with gold the mossy crests of a grove of giant cebias when we rounded a bend to come upon the first ledge of rocks in two days. A low, grassy promontory invited the eyes searching for camping ground. This spot appeared ideal; it certainly was beautiful. The ledge jutted into the river, almost to the opposite shore, forcing the water to rush through a rocky trough into a great foam-spotted pool below.

We could not pitch our tent because the stony ground refused to admit stakes, so we laid the canvas flat. Pepe lunged up the bank with his machete in search of firewood. To my utmost delight I found a little spring of sweet water trickling from the ledge, and by digging a hole was enabled to get a drink, the first good one in more than a week.

A little later, as I was spreading my blankets, George called my attention to shouts up in the woods.

"Pepe's treed something," I said. "Take your gun and hunt him up."

I went on making my bed and busying myself about camp, with little heed of George's departure. Presently, however, I was straightened up by unmistakable shouts of alarm. George and Pepe were yelling in unison, and, from the sound, appeared to be quite a distance away.

"What the deuce!" I ejaculated, snatching up my rifle. I snapped a clip into the magazine, and dropped several loaded clips and a box of extra shells into my coat pocket. After my adventure with the jaguar I had decided never again to find myself short of ammunition. Running up the sloping bank, I entered the forest, shouting for the boys. Answering cries came from in front of me and a little to the left. I could not make out what was said.

Save for drooping moss the forest was comparatively open, and at a hundred paces from the river bank were glades covered with thickets and long grass and short palm trees. The ground sloped upward quite perceptibly.

"Hey there, boys, where are you?" I called.

Pepe's shrill yells mingled with George's shouts. At first their meaning was unintelligible, but after calling twice I got the drift.

"*Javelin*! Go back! *Javelin*! We're treed! Wild pigs! *Santa Maria*! Run for your life!"

This was certainly enlightening and rather embarrassing. I remembered the other time the boys had made me run and I grew hot under the collar.

"I'll be darned if I'll run!" I said in the pride of conceit and wounded vanity. Whereupon I began to climb the slope, stopping every few steps to listen and look. I wondered what had made Pepe go so far for firewood. Still, there was nothing but green wood all about me. Walking round a clump of seared and yellow palms that rustled in the breeze, I suddenly espied George's white shirt. He was in a scrubby sapling not fifteen feet from the ground. Then I discovered Pepe, perched in the forks of a cebia, high above the thickets and low shrubbery. I was scarcely more than a dozen rods from them, down the gradual slope, and both saw me at once.

"Run!!—you Indian, run!" bawled George, waving his hands.

Pepe implored me to fly to save my precious life.

"What for, you darn fools? I don't see anything to run from," I shouted back. My temper had soured a little during the last few days.

"You'd better run or you'll have to climb," replied George. "Wild pigs! A thousand of 'em!"

"Where?"

"Right under us. There! Oh, if they see you! Listen to this." He broke off a branch, trimmed it of leaves, and flung it down. I heard a low trampling roar of many hard little feet, brushings in the thicket, and cracking of twigs. As close as I was, however, I could not see a moving object. The dead grass and brush were several feet high, up to my waist in spots, and, though I changed position several times, no javelin did I see.

"You want to look out! Say, man, these are wild pigs—boars, I tell you! They'll kill you!" bellowed George.

"Are you going to stay up there all night?" I asked, sarcastically.

"We'll stay till they go away."

"All right, I'll scare them away," I replied, and suiting action to word I worked the automatic as fast as it would shoot, aiming into the thicket under George.

Of all the fool things a nettled hunter ever perpetrated that was the worst. A roar answered the echoes of the rifle, and it was a trampling roar, circling round the space bounded by the trees the boys were in. Nervously I clamped a fresh clip of shells into the rifle. Clouds of dust arose, and strange little squeals or grunts sounded seemingly at all points above me. Then the grass and bushes seemed to wave apart and be divided by gray streaks. They were everywhere.

"Run! Run!" shrieked George, high above the tumult.

For a thrilling instant I stood my ground and fired at the bobbing gray backs. But every break made in the ranks by the powerful shells filled in a flash. Before that vicious charge I wavered, then ran as if pursued by demons.

The way was downhill. I tripped, fell, rolled over and over, still clutching my rifle, rose with a bound and fled. The javelin had gained on me. They were at my heels. I ran like a deer. Then, seeing a low branch, I leaped for it, grasped it with one hand, and, crooking an elbow round it, swung with the old giant swing of athletic days.

Hardly before I knew how it happened I was astride a dangerously swaying branch directly over a troop of brownish-gray sharpsnouted, fiendish-eyed little pecaries.

Some were young and sleek, others were old and rough, some had little yellow teeth or tusks, and all pointed their sharp noses upward, as if expecting me to fall into their very mouths. Feeling safe once more, I loaded the rifle and began to kill the biggest, most vicious of the javelin. When I had killed twelve in twelve shots, I saw that shooting a few would be of no avail. There were hundreds, it seemed, and I had scarcely fifty shells left. Moreover, the rifle barrel grew so hot that it burned my hands. Hearing George's yell, I replied, somewhat sheepishly:

"I'm all right, George—only treed. How're you?"

"Pigs all gone—they chased you. Pepe thinks we can risk running."

"Don't take any chances," I yelled in answer to this.

In trying to find a more comfortable posture, so I could apply myself to an interesting study of my captors, I made the startling discovery that the branch which upheld me was splitting from the tree trunk. My heart began to pound in my breast; then it went up into my throat. Every move I made— for I had started to edge toward the tree— widened the little white split.

"Boys, my branch is breaking!" I called, piercingly.

"Can't you get another?" returned George.

"No! I daren't nove! Hurry, boys! If you don't scare these these brutes off I'm a goner!"

My eyes were rivited upon the gap where the branch was slowly separating from the tree trunk. I glanced about me to see if I could not leap to another branch. There was nothing near that would uphold me. In desperation I resolved to drop my rifle, cautiously get to my feet upon the branch, and with one spring try to reach the tree. When I was about to act upon this last chance I heard Pepe's shrill yell and a crashing in the brush. Then followed the unmistakable roar and crackling of fire. Pepe had fired the brush—no, he was making his way toward me, armed with a huge torch.

"Pepe, you'll set the jungle on fire!" I yelled, forgetting what was at stake. I had a horror of forest fire.

The javelin stirred uneasily, ran around

under me, tumbling over one another. When Pepe burst into sight, holding before him long-stemmed palm leaves flaring in hissing flames, the whole pack of pigs bowled away into the forest at break-neck speed.

"By heaven! Pepe, it was a nervy trick." I leaped down, and the branch came with me. George ran to us, his face white, his eyes big. Behind came a roar that I thought might be another drove of javelin till I saw the smoke and flame.

"Boys, the jungle's on fire. Run for the river."

In our hurry we miscalculated the location of the camp, and dashed out of the jungle over a steep bank, along the base of which we had to wade to reach the ledge. Pepe did not appear very much concerned for the burning jungle, and expressed his belief that the fire would not hurt anything but the ticks.

I kept watching the forest back of us as if I expected it to blow up like a powder mine. Nevertheless, I was agreeably disappointed. A cloud of smoke rolled westward; there was a frequent roaring of burning palms, but the forest fire was nothing such as I had feared.

"Boys, we'll have some roast pig tomorrow, I guess there's fire enough up there for that," I remarked.

Just before dark, when we were at supper, a swarm of black mosquitoes swooped upon us. Pepe could not have evinced more fear of angry snakes, and he began to pile green wood and leaves upon the camp fire to make heavy smoke. We finished our meal before they attacked us, and then there was nothing to do but fight. These mosquitoes were very large, black-bodied, with white-barred wings; their sting was as painful as that of a wasp. We went to bed, but it was only to get up again, for the pest could bite through two thicknesses of blanket. The only thing we could do was to sit or stand in the smoke of the camp fire. There we spent a wretched sleepless night, with the blood-thirsty mosquitoes humming about our ears like a swarm of bees. They did not go away till dawn.

We were all haggard and languid, but George's condition showed me the necessity for renewed efforts to get out of the jungle. Pepe appeared heavy and slow, and what was more alarming, he had lost his appetite. We made George a bed on the canvas in the bow of the boat, where he was soon sound asleep. Then Pepe and I took turns at the oars, making five miles an hour. As on the day before, we glided under the shadows of the great moss-twined cypresses, along the muddy banks where crocodiles basked in the sun and gaunt cattle came down to drink. Once we turned a bushy point to startle a large flock of wild turkeys, perhaps thirty-five in number. They had been resting in the cool sand along the river. Some ran up the bank, a half-dozen flew right over the boat, and most of them squatted down as if to evade detection. Thereafter turkeys and ducks and geese became so common as to be monotonous.

About one o'clock we passed a thatched bamboo and palm-leaf hut on the bank. Some naked little Indians ran like wild quail. A disheveled black head peeped out of a door, then swiftly vanished. From there on we met frequently with huts, and at three o'clock sighted a large one situated upon a high bluff. Upon rounding a bend we came suddenly upon an intersecting river. It was twice as large as the Santa Rosa, and flowed swiftly.

"Taumaulipas," said Pepe.

"This must be the beginning of the Panuco," I returned. "I see tarpon rolling. We must be getting somewhere."

George roused out of his sleep and sat up, as interested and pleased as we were. The Panuco River, here formed, was very wide and flowed swiftly over sand bars. The banks were so high that we could see only the tips of the trees. We beached at the foot of the trail below the large hut, and, with Pepe and me lending aid to George, we climbed the steep bluff.

We found a clear space in which were several commodious huts, gardens and flowers, a grassy yard upon which little naked children were playing with tame deer, parrots screeching, and two very kindly disposed and wondering native women. Pepe engaged them in conversation and learned that the village of Panuco was two days and two nights distant by canoe. How many miles or kilometers we could not learn, or whether or not the canoes traveled steadily day and night. We spent an hour there, and we were much refreshed by the hot milk and the chicken and rice soup with which we were served. The women would accept no pay, so we made them presents.

Pepe and George wanted to stay there that night, but I was for hurrying on our way. So we embarked and made perhaps fifteen more miles before time to camp.

But there was no place to camp. The muddy banks were too narrow at the bottom, and too steep to climb to the top. So I bade Pepe and George find as comfortable places as they could on the boat, and I sat down to make a night of it at the oars; I preferred to risk the dangers of the river at night than to spend miserable hours in the mud.

Twilight had scarcely waned into night when the boys were both deep in slumber. Then the strange, dense, tropical night settled down upon me. The oars were almost noiseless and the water gurgled softly from the bow. Overhead the expanse was dark blue with a few palpitating stars. The river was shrouded in gray gloom and the banks were lost in black obscurity. Great fireflies enhanced the darkness. I trusted a good deal to luck in the matter of going right, yet I kept my ear keen for the sound of quickening current, and turned every few strokes to peer sharply into the gloom. I seemed to have little sense of peril, for, though I hit submerged logs and stranded on bars, I kept on unmindful, and by and by lost what anxiety I had felt. The strange wildness of the river at night, the gray veiled space into which I rowed unheeding, began to work upon my mind.

That was a night of nights. All that remained clear were the sounds and the smells, the feeling of the cool mist, the sight of long, dark forest line and a golden moon half hidden by clouds. Striking among these was the trill of river frogs. The trill of a Northern frog is music, but that of these great silver-throated jungle amphibians was more than music. Close at hand one would thrill me with mellow, rich notes, and then from afar would come the answer, a sweet high tenor, wilder than any other wilderness sound, long sustained, dying away till I held my breath to listen.

So the hours passed and the moon went down into the weird shadows and the Southern Cross rose pale and wonderful.

Gradually the stars vanished in a kind of brightening gray, and dawn was at hand. I awoke to the realization of weary arms and back. Morning came with its steely light on the river, the rolling and melting vapors, the flight of ducks and call of birds. The rosy sun brought no cheer this day. When we stopped, George did not leave the boat, and Pepe and I got breakfast in silence. Soon we were once more on the breast of the current.

I slept all the morning and awoke to find Pepe bowed over the oars. Watching him, I fancied he was stronger than on the preceding day, and I was relieved. We passed a long dugout canoe in which were two, half-naked natives poling with their huge paddles. Pepe's inquiry brought the information that we were two days from Panuco.

The river grew wider and long sand bars obstructed our passage. As it was quicksand we could not wade and had to pole off into the channels. This was wearisome work. We met another canoe and were told Panuco was far, far away, many kilometers. Towards night more natives informed us that the village was just around the next bend! I wondered dully whether this was their way of exercising a sense of humor. The stretches of the river were now miles long and the turns seemed interminably far apart. There was no village beyond any particular bend—nothing but bare banks for miles. We went ashore for a meager supper, rested a couple of hours, and about dark shoved off into the current.

I rowed until I gave out, then awakened Pepe. He took the oars and I crawled back to the stern, where I covered my damp, chilly body with a blanket and fell asleep.

A rude hand brought me back from oblivion. Pepe was shouting in Spanish. I heard the soft swish of swift current. Raising myself, I caught the glimmer of glancing water under the lowering moon. Pepe was frantically pushing his oar into the stream in an effort to shove us off a sand bar. As we seemed solidly fixed and in no danger whatever, I calmed Pepe's fears, and we lay down in the boat and slept till morning.

That day was a repetition of the one before, except that it was hotter, wearier, and the stretches of river were longer, and the natives we met in canoes more stolidly ignorant of distance. The mourning of turtledoves almost drove me wild. There were miles and miles of willows, and every tree was fully of melancholy doves. At dusk we halted on a sand bar, too tired to cook a dinner, and sprawled in the warm sand to sleep like logs.

In the morning we brightened a little, for surely just round the bend we would come to Panuco. Pepe rowed faithfully on, and bend after bend lured us with deceit. I was filled with weariness and disgust, so tired I could hardly lift my hand, so sleepy I could scarcely keep my eyes open. I hated the wide, glassy stretches of river and the muddy banks and dusty cattle.

At noon, when we came unexpectedly upon a cluster of thatched huts to find they made up the village of Panuco, I was sick, for I had expected a little town where we could get some drinking water, and hire a launch to speed us down to Tampico. This appeared little more than other places we had passed, and I climbed up the bank wearily thinking of the long fifty miles we still had to go.

But Panuco was bigger and better than it looked from the river. We found a clean, comfortable inn where we dined well, and learned, to our joy, that a coach left in an hour for Tamos to meet the five o'clock train to Tampico.

We hired a *mozo* to row the boat to Tampico and, carrying our lighter things, we boarded the coach and behind six mules were soon bowling over a good level road.

It was then that the spirit of my mood changed. The gloom faded away as I had seen the mist clouds dissolve in the morning sunlight. It was the end of another wild trip, which I suddenly found had not been so bad after all. As rest from weary labor and assurance of a safe escape from the wilderness became certainties I began that strange and inevitable longing for another trip some day. That feeling grew with the hours and miles. When the little palm-thatched village of Tamos came in sight the sun was setting, and into the rose and golden sky a flock of flamingoes winged regular and beautiful flight, leaving me a thrilling reminder of the lonely jungle river.